SPLIT

USA TODAY BESTSELLING AUTHOR

ALICIA RADES

Published by Crystallite Publishing.
Edited by Melanie Williams.
Cover design by Orina Kafe.

To all the girls who couldn't decide.

CHAPTER 1

I stared down into the jewelry box, knowing this was the hardest decision I ever had to make. On one end of the box sat an angel wing pendant with a chain attached. The opposite section held a hand-made bracelet with a treble clef charm wove into the purple string. Each one represented one of the men I loved. Each one was a reminder that I had to choose between them or I'd lose them both.

These two pieces of jewelry were the only ones I owned apart from the two studs in my ears and the ring shaped like a rose I'd bought on a whim a year ago, before all this started. I only remembered I had it a few weeks ago when I opened my great grandmother's jewelry box to deposit my two birthday presents. There it sat wedged in the ring slot that ran through the middle of the box.

My eyes locked on the angel wing necklace. *Aaron, I'll choose him,* I thought. My gaze drifted to the music bracelet. *No, I should choose Logan.* I rested my face in my hands and glanced between the two beautiful pieces of jewelry. Why did

I have to choose between them? Why couldn't I keep them both?

"Maddie?" a voice called my name.

I jerked in my seat and slammed my right knee against the underside of my desk. My heart rate slowed when I noticed it was only Alaina. She stood in my doorway dressed in her typical jeans and solid swoop-neck tee. A headband—her signature hairpiece—wrapped around her skull. Today, it was burgundy to match her shirt. Her stick-straight brunette hair fell to her shoulders, and her expression read curiosity.

"Don't you knock?" I teased after I had a moment to relax.

My best friend inched her way into my room and crossed over to my queen-sized bed. She tossed her purse, printed with Van Gogh's *Starry Night*, onto the mattress. "I did knock. And rang the doorbell. And knocked again."

She plopped down at the end of the bed next to my cat, Parrot. It was the worst name for a cat, but my sisters and I had named him when we were little. He got his name because every time we talked, he'd meow back at us like he was "parroting" us. Now he just sat around and didn't make a sound. He could have easily been mistaken for a thick towel.

Alaina petted his ragdoll fur and then looked up at me. "No one answered, but I knew you had to be home, so I let myself in."

I twisted in my chair to face her, rubbing my aching knee. "It's okay. Maybe the doorbell is broken or something."

It probably wasn't. I'd been so spacey lately that there was a good chance I didn't hear it. It was the Monday before the first day of school—my senior year—so my parents were at work. Both of my sisters, Kayla and Amy, had already moved into their college dorms last weekend, so I had the whole house to myself for the next week.

"It looks like you're still having trouble deciding," Alaina pointed out, gesturing to my jewelry box.

A blush rose to my cheeks. "To be honest, I don't want to."

She picked at her fingernails and shrugged. "Then don't."

"What?" I nearly choked. "They told me if I don't decide by the time school starts I don't get either of them."

"So, they're just both going to move on like that?" Alaina snapped her fingers when she said the word *that*.

I absentmindedly scanned the room in thought. "I guess so. I have to choose. I'd rather have one of them than neither of them."

"Then choose. You've had a whole week to think about it since they gave you the ultimatum."

"It's not that simple, Alaina," I complained, burying my face in my hands. She wasn't exactly helping. "I've thought about it and thought about it, and the truth is, I'm in love with both of them." I dropped my hands and sucked in a deep breath.

She narrowed her eyes in skepticism. "You can't be in love with two people at once."

Alaina would never understand. She and Jordan had been dating ever since freshman year. She never had eyes for anyone else and never gave another guy a chance. She would never know how it felt for your heart to ache for one man as equally as it did for another. She wouldn't understand how picturing a future with one guy could fill you with such happiness only to simultaneously cause pain when you realized that future didn't include the other.

"Go with Logan," Alaina told me. She'd said the same thing at least three times in the last week.

"But," I countered, "I don't know if he's the right choice."

"Then choose Aaron."

"I don't know if he's the right choice, either!"

"Well, let's look at this logically." She shifted on my purple comforter to cross her legs. "What are the pros and cons of each guy?"

I shrugged. "Everything about both of them is good."

She pressed her lips together. "Well, if you choose Aaron, at least your families will get along."

"Okay," I agreed. "That's a pro for Aaron."

Aaron's family and I went way back. Our moms had been friends since high school. We grew up playing together at the park and attending each other's birthday parties. We hadn't talked much since the start of junior high school, though. It wasn't until his brother, Chris, graduated college last December that we got to talking again at Chris's graduation party. Aaron had asked for my number, and we'd been texting ever since.

"But then again," Alaina pointed out, "at least Logan is part of our group."

Logan and I had started talking around the same time last year. His two best friends, who were twins, moved away over Christmas break, and our friend Emily invited him to sit by us at lunch. We grew close, and I fell for him. The only problem was that I was falling for Aaron at the same time.

I sighed. "Okay, a point for both. I wish they didn't make me have to choose!"

I would never forget the meeting we had last week. Logan invited me out for lunch, only when I reached the café, both he and Aaron were waiting for me.

"What's this?" I'd asked. I plastered on a smile like seeing the two of them side-by-side didn't bother me.

Aaron smiled back, but Logan's face remained expressionless.

"Maddie," Aaron said with a sigh, "we need to talk."

I wasn't sure if my heart stopped or raced, but my fingers quivered as I slid into the bench across from them. The red leather squeaked as I sat.

"It's time to choose," Logan had said. Even though I couldn't read his expression, my heart fluttered in response to the way he looked at me. Even behind his glasses, his blue eyes were breathtaking.

"Choose? Like, choose an entrée?" I feigned. I reached for the menu at our table and flipped it open, except I could already sense where this was going.

"No." Logan gently closed the menu on me, pulling my attention back to him. "We mean, it's time to choose between us."

My heart dropped. Choose between them? But that meant someone would get hurt.

"It's not fair to any of us," Aaron told me. His gaze locked on mine from under dark lashes, and for a moment, the café seemed to disappear. He had perfectly symmetrical features with brown eyes you could get lost in and a to-die-for smile with a dimple on the left side. My insides warmed when I looked at him.

Logan nodded in agreement. I caught the movement out of the corner of my eye and immediately forced my gaze off Aaron. Only, looking at Logan didn't help slow my heart rate. Although he wasn't as physically attractive as Aaron, having a smaller build and unkempt blond hair that fell into his eyes, something about him turned my insides to mush—in a good way—every time I saw him.

I stared down at the menu in front of me. They were both right. I *wasn't* being fair, but that didn't make the decision any easier.

"Neither of us wants to be the *other guy*, Maddie," Logan stated.

My gut twisted, causing me to lose the appetite I had when I walked into the café. "I don't want to lose either of you," I managed in a whisper, but my eyes remained locked on the image of freshly brewed coffee on the front page of the menu.

"Neither of us want to lose you, either," Aaron promised. "But eventually, you can only end up with one of us. The other can't move on until we know who you've chosen."

"Hey," Logan said soothingly. He shifted in an attempt to get me to look at him. I finally did, but it didn't help with the whole insides-turning-to-mush thing. "It's clear we both have feelings for you and that you feel something back. But we can't keep sharing you."

My mouth hung open slightly. As soon as I noticed, I snapped it shut. It wasn't like I was *dating* either of them. I mean, sure, I'd hung out with them both and we texted a lot, but I wasn't fooling around with them or anything.

I swallowed hard. "Do I have to choose right now?" My voice came out so small that I wasn't sure they even heard me. It felt like my heart was ripping in two, one half longing for Logan while the other reached toward Aaron.

They both exchanged a glance.

"We can give you two weeks," Logan told me. "By the time school starts, you'll have to choose one of us."

I took a deep breath to stall, but eventually, I had to force myself to speak. "What if I can't decide by then?" I blinked several times to keep the tears at bay.

"Then we're both moving on," Aaron said with confidence, a trait I greatly admired in him. "It's not fair to lead us on like this."

When I couldn't bring myself to say anything else, they

both stood and exited the café. It was like they had a mutual agreement to abandon me at a calculated moment so their words would sink in. Logan went left while Aaron headed right, and in that moment, my heart split in two.

Alaina's voice pulled me back to the present. "You still have a week left."

"You're right." I twisted around in my chair to face the jewelry box again. The angel wing pendant dangled delicately from its chain when I lifted it. "I just don't know if a week will make any difference." I fastened the chain around my neck and looked into the mirror on my wall to test how I felt with it on. The corners of my lips twitched up as I thought of Aaron.

Alaina stood from the bed and situated herself behind me to view my reflection. "It looks pretty on you."

My hand came up to gently touch the charm. My reflection stared back at me with sad brown eyes, the bags under them an indication of the toll this decision was taking on me. My dark hair was pulled into a messy bun that needed some serious help, and my pale skin had gone make-up free for the past several days. I hadn't worked up the courage to leave the house and talk to Logan or Aaron yet, not before I made my decision.

I reached toward the jewelry box again and pulled the purple music bracelet out of it. "Can you help?" I held my wrist out to Alaina.

She agreed with a friendly smile. "How's that?" She tugged at the strings slightly to test how tight it was.

"It's fine, thanks." I looked into the mirror again and rested my knuckles on my chin to see how I felt about Logan's gift. It was perfect, or at least it would be if I wasn't distracted by the angel wing necklace hanging across my chest.

I pursed my lips in frustration. "Forget it. I can't decide right now. Can we talk about something else?"

Alaina returned to her spot on my bed, and I leaned my elbow against the back of my chair to face her.

"I met this guy at the flea market yesterday who was really interested in my paintings," she told me excitedly.

"Oh, awesome! How much did you make?"

Her lips twisted in disappointment. "He didn't want to *buy* them."

I scoffed. "Typical."

Alaina laughed, and I joined in. When she finally composed herself, she continued her story. "He said I was really talented and told me about this art night the library is hosting in a couple of weeks. It's this thing where people from the community display their work, and at the end they hand out prizes. There's even a chance someone might buy my art. They're holding an opening night party where people can come in and look at the art. Then over the next week, the community gets to vote on which ones they like best."

"That sounds awesome! How come I've never heard of it before?"

She shrugged. "I guess this is the first year they're doing it."

"Maybe I should enter some of my drawings," I suggested.

"If you want to. The deadline is soon, so you better get drawing."

"I might have something I could use. You always seem to meet the coolest people at the flea market."

Alaina smiled. I knew she really enjoyed going, and it was a great way for her to earn some extra cash on her paintings. It wasn't much, but it was better than nothing.

"Well, if you wanted to sell some of your drawings, we could split the cost of a space," she suggested.

I fell silent for a beat while considering her offer. "I don't know. I don't feel like I'm good enough to sell my art." It was one thing to display it for fun. It was another to ask money for it. My drawings meant more to me than almost anything, which made it difficult to accept the idea that someone might find as much value in them as I did. I didn't want to jump into selling them before I knew they were the best they could possibly be. Besides, it's not like I could sell my drawings to just anyone. They deserved to go to someone who really appreciated them.

Alaina rolled her eyes. "Whatever. You're great. If you joined me, you'd get a kick out of some of the crazies."

"The crazies?" I asked warily.

She laughed. "Oh, we don't get them often, but yesterday I had a psychic come look at my paintings. She runs that little shop downtown."

My brows shot up. "A psychic, huh?"

"She said one of my paintings looked pretty mystical and would look good in her shop."

"So, she bought it?" I asked hopefully.

Alaina smiled like she was trying not to laugh. "Do they ever? No, but she gave me her card and said I might need it."

"I'm sure you will." The sarcasm was heavy in my tone.

"Well, maybe you could use it."

"Me?"

Alaina wiggled her eyebrows. "Yeah. Maybe she could tell you which guy you'll end up with."

"It'd be easier than trying to decide on my own," I admitted.

"Well." She dragged out the word.

"What? You're not suggesting…?"

Her expression lit up. "Why not? You won't listen to me. And girl, you really need to get out of the house."

I turned back to my reflection and silently scrutinized my disheveled appearance. I did need to get out, and I could use a sign of some sort.

"No, Alaina. I'm not turning to some *psychic*. You know I don't believe in that stuff."

She rolled her eyes again. "Well, of course not. It's just for fun. And her shop is just down the street from that Chinese buffet you love."

I shot out of my seat and grabbed my bath towel from the hook on the back of my door. "Say no more! I'll do anything for orange chicken. Let me take a quick shower."

I rummaged through my dresser for a clean outfit before exiting the room. Alaina's laughter echoed down the hall on my way to the bathroom.

After clicking the door shut, I removed my necklace and bracelet. The hot water soothed my nerves slightly, but they quickly returned when I stepped out of the shower and spotted the two pieces of jewelry on the countertop. I dressed and brushed my hair into a high wet ponytail and then shoved the jewelry in my jeans pocket. I found Alaina waiting for me in the living room, fiddling with her phone on the couch.

"Ready?" she asked when I made it down the stairs.

"Yep, just let me get my shoes."

We climbed into Alaina's car a few minutes later. I didn't really care about the psychic thing—I was only doing it to get a ride to the Chinese restaurant—but for a brief moment, I hoped that somehow this psychic could make my heart whole again.

CHAPTER 2

Alaina and I pulled up to a small shop that read "Psychic Advisor" in the window and advertised crystal ball and palm readings. I'd noticed the place before but never paid much attention to it. It sat in an older part of our small town where all the shops were smashed together and had apartments above them. That left little parking out front. Apparently no one wanted to park in front of the psychic's shop, though, because we found a spot waiting for us.

"I think the world can sense this psychic is crazy," I joked about the parking.

"Oh, stop it," Alaina scolded, swatting at me lightly while an amused smile crossed her face. "It's just for kicks. Now get your butt in there or I'm not taking you to the buffet."

I slumped out of the car and took a cautious step forward. Before I reached the door, I turned to Alaina to make sure she was coming.

She threw her purse over her shoulder and locked the car

with the key fob in her hand. "I'm coming." I could almost hear the laughter in her voice, like she thought it was hilarious to see me turning to a psychic for help.

"This is crazy," I muttered before pulling the door open.

"Well, you need someone to make a decision for you."

I let out a puff of air and entered the shop. Shades of purple and pink hit me as we walked in. Shelves of tarot cards, books on psychic practice, and magic kits lined one wall while dream catchers of all colors and sizes took up space on another. A couple of crystal balls sat on display on the far wall, and candles lined a small table in front of us. The checkout counter stood in the back left corner of the shop, and a doorway covered by a curtain of pink and purple beads interrupted the flow of shelving on the right. The whole place smelled strongly of lemongrass incense. It all seemed over the top to me.

Alaina picked up one of the candles and gave it a big whiff. She let out a breath of satisfaction before shoving it in my face.

"Yuck!" I pulled away instantly. "What is that?"

She checked the label and shrugged. "Chamomile. It smells good."

I turned up my nose the same time I heard the beads in the doorway jingle as they bounced off one another. A smiling woman who looked to be in her early thirties stepped into the room. Her curly strawberry blond hair fell to her shoulders, and she wore slim blue jeans and a pale green shirt. If this was the psychic, she was totally not what I was expecting. She looked so *normal*.

"Can I help you ladies with something?" She spoke in a soft, calming tone.

A brief silence passed before Alaina spoke. "My friend wants a psychic reading."

"Well, I can certainly help with that. I'm Chloe." She extended her hand, and I warily shook it.

"Madelyn." I cleared my throat before clarifying. "Maddie." *If she's psychic, shouldn't she already know my name?*

"And you're the painter," Chloe greeted, shaking Alaina's hand.

"Yep." She smiled. "I'm Alaina. Any chance you're ready for that painting?"

Chloe let out a light laugh. "Honestly, I'm not sure I have the room for it." She gestured around the shop, which didn't have a free inch of space anywhere on the walls. "So, you're interested in a reading?" she asked, turning back to me.

I resisted the urge to roll my eyes. There's no way this lady was psychic. She didn't even play the part well. Alaina elbowed me in the ribs when I didn't answer.

"Yep," I managed to say, playing along.

"Well, if it's okay with you two, I'll have Alaina stay out here, and I can give you a reading in the other room."

I exchanged a quick glance with Alaina. "I guess that's okay."

I nervously followed behind Chloe and through the beaded curtain. This room wasn't much different from the one I'd just been standing in, though it was smaller and didn't have a window. Hues of pink and purple blanketed the space, and soft lighting gave off a mysterious vibe. A round table with two chairs stood in the middle of the floor, and a crystal ball sat on top. I did my best not to burst out laughing. It's like she was trying to cater to pre-teen girls who were still infatuated by unicorns and glitter.

"Please, take a seat." Chloe gestured to one of the chairs. "We won't need this." She picked up her crystal ball and moved it to another table in the corner, which held a collection of neatly-situated framed photographs.

I eyed the photos. The one to the furthest left showed Chloe in a graduation uniform. Another showed her in what looked like a rainforest surrounded by a group of indigenous people. In another, she stood in front of a large building that looked like a temple of some sort.

"You travel a lot?" I asked in an attempt to ease the awkwardness. If anything, it only fueled the tension in the air.

"Yes." Chloe smiled, glancing at the photographs. "These photos document my journey to where I am today." She spoke slowly like time didn't matter to her.

I should have kept my mouth shut.

Chloe sat across from me. "During college, I spent some time traveling, learning about ancient religions and cultures. It taught me a lot about spiritualism and gave me the chance to explore so much about the universe."

By "universe," did she mean this psychic thing? She couldn't actually believe she was psychic. Or maybe she spent her time learning how to deceive others into believing it. *Well, it's not going to work on me*, I thought. *I'm only doing this to appease Alaina.*

"Eventually, I decided to return home," she continued. "What better way to use that knowledge than helping people?"

This was her idea of helping people?

"So, uh, how does this work?" I asked, hoping to get this over with as soon as possible. My gaze shifted around the room. I spotted a couple of open spaces where Alaina's painting could hang if Chloe actually bought it.

Chloe's sweet smile returned. "That depends on what you're interested in. I can give you a palm reading or a tarot card reading. We can talk about your past, present, or future. I sense you're here about your future, Maddie."

Easy guess. I was a teen girl. Of course I was curious about my future.

"You're here about a boy, aren't you?"

I gave her an uncertain smile and nodded. Another easy guess.

"Oh," she said with surprise. "Two boys?"

Now *that* was a lucky guess. Or maybe Alaina had talked to her about me already. I nodded again.

"Ooh. Tell me about them." Her slow, calming voice began to sound more normal, like we were best friends spilling our secrets at a slumber party.

"Well." I dragged out the word, unsure of what to say to her. If I didn't say much, I could test just how much of a psychic she was.

Next, she'll probably say something like, "I'm getting an 'A' name," and I'll say something like, "Alex!" and she'll be like, "Right, Alex," and I'll be like, "Fraud! I don't know an Alex. His name is Aaron."

I laughed at myself internally, really starting to feel my mischievous evil side emerging. But I couldn't bring myself to be that mean, so I decided to play along instead for both Chloe and Alana's sake.

"They're both pretty good," I told her vaguely.

"Maddie, I'm getting the sense that you have a big decision to make."

Again, what teenage girl my age wasn't stressing over some big decision? For some girls my age, it was what car they were going to buy for their eighteenth birthday, and for others, it was already about which college they'd attend next year. For me, it was which guy I wanted to spend my senior year with—and hopefully long after.

"Yep. Big decisions." I hoped I didn't come off sounding too unimpressed.

"And this decision has to do with these two boys?" She smiled at me again, easing some of my anxiety.

"You're good," I complimented, but I was totally bluffing. These were easy guesses. They would have been even easier if Alaina had said something to her about me. Maybe that's why she made Alaina sit outside, so she wouldn't realize Chloe was a fraud.

"So, your heart belongs to two men," Chloe mused thoughtfully, not even looking at me now. "Tell me how you feel about them."

What, was she some type of therapist now? *And how does that make you feel?*

I shrugged, but I'd already told myself I'd play along. As soon as the boys entered my mind, Chloe and the shop seemed to fade away. I stared into the distance as I spoke. "Well, one of them is smart, and he's a really good musician. He makes me feel safe and comfortable when I'm around him, you know?" I paused for a moment, forcing my heart to slow after picturing Logan in my mind. "The other guy makes me laugh and brings out a side of me that I really enjoy. He really cares about me, too." The butterflies in my stomach sprang to life when I thought about Aaron. *Calm down, girl,* I told myself. *You could give yourself a heart attack the way you react when they're both on your mind.* "They're both very different, but in their own way, they both bring out the best in me. And strangely, I think I bring out the best in them. One calls me his muse. The other calls me his angel."

"And you? Do you have a nick name for either of them?"

"No," I answered, still staring off into space where I could picture their faces in my mind.

"Well, Maddie."

The sound of my name pulled me out of my daydream, and I looked back at Chloe.

"I can tell that you love both of them very much. It's written all over your face when you talk about them." She pressed her lips together in thought. "I may be able to help you."

Just tell me which guy I end up with, I silently begged, even though I was sure she couldn't read my mind or tell the future.

Chloe sat up a little bit straighter. "Here's what we can do. Since you obviously love both of them, why don't you choose them both?"

What a load of crap, I thought, but I kept my cool. "I can't choose both of them. They told me I have to choose or they'll both move on."

"Ah," she said with a gleam in her eyes, "but they'll be none the wiser. You see, how this works is that you can have both boys. You can live a life with both of them, but it will feel like you only chose one."

"I don't understand. What's the point in that?"

Chloe leaned in closer across the table. "Think of it like alternate universes. One single decision will split your heart in two. One half of your heart will go one way and live in a universe with the first boy. The other half of your heart will live in a world with the second boy."

"Split my heart?" I asked warily. She made it sound like I'd be placing my beating heart on a butcher's table. I still wasn't sure I understood, and I'd never been great at following those alternate universe sci-fi movies.

"Do you happen to have something that belongs to the boys with you?"

I was ready to shake my head when I realized I still had their jewelry in my pocket. I could hardly believe my luck. I dug into my jeans and pulled out the necklace and bracelet and set them on the table in front of me. What exactly did she have in mind?

Chloe stared down at them like I'd just placed a bag of diamonds in front of her. "This is perfect." She held onto each one in a separate hand and placed them behind her back. "Maddie, in a moment, I'm going to ask you to choose a piece of jewelry. Whatever decision you make, you will also choose the other, allowing you to live a life with both boys."

I still wasn't following her logic, but it didn't matter because I didn't believe her anyway. At the same time, I liked the idea of choosing a boy at random. It was the best solution anyone had come up with by this point, so I figured I'd go with it and be happy with whichever decision I made. I couldn't keep dragging this out. It didn't matter whether I made my decision today or next week; someone was still going to get hurt. So, I'd have to settle with random.

"Okay," Chloe announced once she'd mixed the jewelry up in her hands. She stuck two fists out toward me, and I eyed them. She began chanting something incoherent under her breath, but a second later, she went abruptly silent and pulled back slightly. "Wait. I must warn you that if you change your mind about the boy you choose, you risk losing them both. Do you understand?"

The look in her eyes made it seem like she was warning

me of my own death. She was taking this *way* too seriously, but I nodded anyway. Then I took a deep breath to prepare myself for the big reveal. Which hand would I choose, and which boy's jewelry lay inside?

Chloe extended her fists again. "So, which boy will it be? Logan, or Aaron?"

CHAPTER 3
LOGAN

"How'd it go?" Alaina asked in a high pitched teasing voice when we exited the shop.

My cheeks flamed. Finally, I had made a decision. I mean, Chloe's whole "splitting my heart" spiel was a load of crap, but at least I'd chosen someone. She didn't make me pay, so I didn't feel so bad about coming to a psychic.

"I have a feeling you'll be back," she'd said when I tried to pay her for her time. I wasn't going to argue and make her take my money since I didn't have much to begin with.

I fingered the bracelet around my wrist and barely noticed the smile that crossed my face. I didn't answer Alaina's question until I slid into the passenger seat. "She helped me make a choice." The smile on my face spread wider.

Alaina started the car. "So, what'd she do? Look into her crystal ball and see which guy you'd end up with?"

I laughed as we drove along the street. "No. She was a complete fake, but she made me pick one at random. I figured it was the best way to go about it. And you know what? I'm happy with my decision."

One of Alaina's brows shot up. "Who'd you choose, then?"

I glanced down at the bracelet and smiled again. "Logan."

"Good. I'm happy for you. Is that buffet on this street or the next one?"

"It's just past the next stop light," I told her.

It wasn't long before we found a parking spot.

"By the way," I said as we walked toward the restaurant. "Did you and Chloe talk about me before we went there?"

"What? No."

"Oh," was all I said before I entered the restaurant and became distracted by the delicious aroma.

"How are you going to tell them?" Alaina asked in the car on our way back to my house from lunch.

I shrugged. "I think I should sleep on it, just to make sure. I'll text them tomorrow morning and see if they're available to meet up."

"Sounds like a plan. Can I be there to see Aaron's reaction?" She looked at me sideways before fixing her eyes back on the road. She couldn't hide the grin creeping onto her face.

I swatted at her playfully. "No, you can't. Don't be so mean to him. Just because I'm not picking him doesn't mean I don't like him anymore. He's still a good person."

It had never been a secret that Alaina preferred Logan over Aaron. Logan was one of our friends, and Aaron was too popular for her.

"Oh, come on. It'll be great," she teased, but I wasn't

amused. I didn't want to hurt Aaron, but I didn't have any other option.

We pulled into my driveway a couple of minutes later. "You're so lucky to have a car," I told Alaina on our way to the front door.

I had access to a car over the summer when Kayla and Amy were around, but now that they were off at two different colleges, they'd taken *both* our extra vehicles with them. Mom and Dad said that if I wanted a car, I needed to get a job to pay for the insurance first like my sisters did. I'd been looking, but there weren't a lot of open opportunities for someone under eighteen in our small town. My parents didn't even want to hire me at their real estate company.

"You know that if you ever need a car, you can borrow mine, right?" Alaina told me.

"Yeah."

It's not like I really *needed* a car anyway. Pretty much everything in town was within walking or biking distance, and if I needed to head out of town, Alaina was always willing to give me a ride.

We headed to my bedroom, where Parrot unsurprisingly hadn't moved from his spot on my bed.

"What now?" Alaina asked.

I dropped Aaron's angel necklace into my jewelry box, briefly wondering if I should give it back to him. Then I turned my attention to my wrist and admired Logan's bracelet. It was perfect. How could I not see that before?

I shrugged in response to Alaina's question. "I have some watercolors if you want to play around with them."

She shrugged back. "Sounds good."

I gathered some painting supplies for Alaina and grabbed the new set of pencils my parents had given me for my seventeenth birthday. We sat in the chairs on my back patio and practiced our art. Alaina painted an image of the flowers lining the fence in my backyard while I sketched Logan's face. Placing my pencil to the paper was unlike anything else. It filled me with a sense of comfort and pride. As Logan's features began to take shape inside the sketchbook, another wave of bliss overcame me.

The sun shone bright above us. We talked about boys and the upcoming school year until my parents arrived home. They'd brought home Italian takeout.

"How'd we know you'd be here, Alaina?" my mother joked when Alaina and I entered the kitchen. She balanced gracefully on her high heels and leaned across the table to unload her bag. "We brought extra for you."

"Aww, that's really sweet of you, Mrs. Rose, but I think my parents would prefer I eat at home for once. I was actually going to head home pretty soon."

"Okay, drive safe," my mom told her.

Alaina gathered her purse and keys. Her latest painting was already dry and in her hands. "Bye, Maddie."

I pulled her into a hug. "Bye. See you later."

A moment after Alaina exited the kitchen, the sound of the door clicking behind her reached my ears.

"What'd you two do all day?" my dad asked as he loosened his tie. He hated the darn thing but insisted on wearing it day in and day out. It was part of the job, he said.

"Well, Dad, if you really want to know, we're part of an illegal drug cartel, and we spent the day painting pictures so we can hide the drugs inside the canvas and smuggle them across the border."

My father's eyes widened.

"Dad, I'm kidding." I rolled my eyes and took a seat at the table.

"Well, yeah," he said flatly. "That was obvious." He tossed his tie onto the kitchen counter and smoothed down his brown hair. It was beginning to gray around the edges. I'd suggested he dye it, but he thought it made him look more sophisticated and experienced. Whatever.

"Seriously, we just hung out and drew and stuff." I shrugged. "We went out for lunch." My parents wouldn't know the difference if I had left the house or not, but it's not like I was irresponsible and would go behind their backs or anything. "By the way, I'm planning to meet up with Logan and Aaron again tomorrow. That's okay, right?" They didn't mind, as long as I told them where I was going and didn't bring a guy back to the house when they weren't around.

My mother sighed as she settled into the chair across from me. "You can't keep leading the poor boys on, Maddie."

"I know. That's why I'm meeting with them."

She eyed me curiously. "Okay. Can we say a blessing on the food?"

After dinner, I escaped to my room and checked my phone. Neither Logan nor Aaron had texted me all week. My parents would probably be surprised when they received our phone bill next month. They wouldn't know what to think about such a sharp decline in texts.

I didn't send the text yet, though. Everything about Logan felt *right*, but asking them to meet with me still made me nervous every time I thought about it. I pulled out my sketchbook again and flipped to the page I'd been drawing of Logan.

Yes, I'm sure he's the right choice. I'm his muse, and he... well, he brings me to life.

I lay in bed that night redefining Logan's features in the drawing. I focused on his soft jawline and straight nose. I loved the way his hair curled up at the ends, and I accented that in the image. His eyes I could never get right, though. It was like in real life they shone brighter than I could represent in a drawing.

I fell asleep that night thinking about Logan and the future we'd have together.

By the time I woke up, the sun was shining brightly into my room, and I wasn't as nervous about contacting Logan and Aaron. My parents had already left for work. I headed downstairs and poured myself a bowl of cereal. Parrot rubbed his body against my leg affectionately.

"You already have food in your bowl," I told him.

He looked up at me and meowed. Right. He could see the *bottom* of his dish. To him, that meant he didn't have any food left. I gave in and poured him some extra food, and he quietly dug in while I settled myself into a chair at the table.

I pulled my phone out while eating and sent the text I'd been dreading. My fingers didn't quiver like they had every time I thought about it last night. In fact, I wasn't even worried at this point. My body completely relaxed, and I knew I'd made the right decision.

Made a decision. Can we meet for lunch?

I sent the text to both of them and quickly received a reply from Logan. He was a go. Before I finished my cereal, Aaron also texted back saying he was available. I stared down at

Aaron's text slightly heartbroken. It's not that I thought I'd made the wrong choice; I just knew it was going to hurt him.

I thought about dressing up to some extent, but I had to remind myself that this wasn't a date. Instead, I wore my typical jeans and tee and brushed my dark hair into a high ponytail. I added some mascara and lip gloss, but that was it.

I still had several hours until lunch and didn't know what to do with myself, so I clicked on the TV and opened my sketchbook to a new page. When Parrot crossed through the living room, I called to him to sit by me, but he ignored me and ran up the stairs to sleep on my bed.

"Sure," I called to him. "You only love me when you want food."

I turned back to my drawing just before I heard the buzz of my phone. My heart leapt in my chest. Was it Logan? I opened the message to find it was Alaina asking what our plans were for the day. I texted her back, telling her that if she wanted to hang out, it'd have to be after lunch. The minutes seemed to tick by slowly as I waited to meet up with the boys. As noon approached, my pulse quickened. I couldn't tell if I was nervous or excited. It was probably a combination of both. Eventually, I gave up the wait and flipped my sketchbook closed. I pulled my bicycle out of the garage and rode to the café. I arrived early even though I'd tried to pedal slower than normal. Neither of them were there yet, so I sat at a table by myself.

The waitress, a girl named Laura, came to my table while I was still sitting alone.

"Are you ready to order, or do you need a few minutes?" she asked.

I knotted my hands in my lap. "I'm waiting for some people. Can I start with a water?"

"Sure thing." She retreated from my table the same time Aaron entered the café.

My nerves sprang to life again, and I anxiously waved him over. He wore an empty expression, like he wasn't sure what to feel yet. Honestly, it didn't bother me as much as I thought it would. It'd be easy for him to get over me and find another girl.

He pulled out the chair across from me and sat. "So, we're alone. What does that mean?" His tone was as hard to read as his face.

"Don't worry. Logan is coming, too. I wanted to tell you together."

Laura returned with my water. "Can I get you something to drink?" she asked Aaron.

He smiled up at her. "Water is fine, thanks." His gaze returned to mine, and I was surprised when I didn't feel my normal blush rise to my cheeks. I really had made the right choice.

Logan entered the café before Laura made it back with Aaron's water. He spotted us right away. He gave a friendly smile when he sat in the chair next to Aaron, but again, it was like he didn't know what to expect. I couldn't blame him.

"Will anyone else be joining you?" Laura asked. She was probably annoyed by running back and forth for water.

"No, this is it," I told her.

"And can I get you anything to drink?" she addressed Logan.

He shook his head. "No, thanks. I'm fine."

That seemed odd considering he usually ordered a soda. As soon as I thought it, I realized he was probably preparing for a quick exit in case he wasn't the guy I chose.

"Do you need a few more minutes, then?" she asked.

"Yes, please," I answered.

"So." Aaron got right to the chase. "Who's it going to be?"

I didn't even need to take a deep breath to calm myself. I was confident in my decision. I reached for my water glass, finally revealing the bracelet around my wrist. Aaron had to do a double take, and a smile formed across Logan's face.

I didn't have to think twice about announcing it. "I choose Logan."

Aaron chewed the side of his lip and nodded like he understood, but I couldn't miss the tension in his jaw. He stood.

"Aaron," I tried, but it was no use.

"It's okay, Maddie," he said in a tone that didn't reflect the anger in his face. He stood behind his chair, gripping onto the back of it tightly. "You know why? Because one day, you're going to realize that *this*," he gestured between himself and me, "was meant to be. Eventually, you'll realize that we should be together. And I'll wait for you because you're worth it."

And then he turned and exited the café. I swallowed the disappointment rising in my throat. I didn't like hurting him like that, but as my eyes drifted back to Logan's beaming face, I knew I'd made the right choice. Aaron was wrong. I wasn't supposed to be with him. I was supposed to be with Logan.

CHAPTER 4

AARON

I parted the beaded curtains and thought about what Chloe had just said to me. The lady was completely unconvincing, but at least I finally made a decision. She refused to take my money, saying she had a feeling I'd be back sometime. I didn't feel bad about getting the session free. I found Alaina admiring the dream catchers nearby, but we didn't say anything until we exited the shop.

"How'd it go?" she asked with raised eyebrows.

I couldn't help but blush. "I made a decision."

"That's great! What'd she do? Look into her crystal ball?"

I laughed as I settled into the passenger seat. "Not exactly. I chose at random, and honestly, I'm happy with my decision."

"Oh? So who's the lucky guy?"

I pulled the angel wing charm away from my body to look at it. "Aaron."

We drove slowly along the street.

"Well, that's good," Alaina said. "Your family will love him."

I let the smile that was fighting its way onto my face win. "Yeah, they will."

"Is the buffet on this street or the next one?"

"It's past that stop light. By the way, did you and Chloe talk about me?"

Alaina glanced sideways at me. "No. What would make you say that?"

I shrugged without answering, but I wasn't sure I believed Alaina. Hadn't Chloe mentioned Logan's and Aaron's names? I tried to remember if I'd said their names out loud, but I couldn't recall my exact words. Either Alaina was lying to me or Chloe was the real deal. Or maybe I just had a bad memory. What did it matter at this point, though? I'd made a decision, and that's what this whole "psychic reading" thing was supposed to accomplish.

"Mm." Alaina pulled into a parking space at the Chinese restaurant. "Can't wait for the egg rolls."

We returned home and headed to my room, where I placed Logan's bracelet in my jewelry box. Would he want it back? After all, he'd hand made it. I didn't want all that work to go to waste. If anyone understood how much work went into a good piece of art like that, it was me.

"So, how are you going to tell them?" Alaina asked, plopping down onto my bed.

"I think I'll text them tomorrow morning and ask them to meet up. I want to tell them together."

"Sounds like a plan. Do you want me to be there?"

I sat next to her. "Is there a reason you should be?"

She sighed. "Logan's probably going to want someone to talk to when you break the news to him. He's my friend, too, you know. And Jordan and his family are still at their cabin up north, so I really have nothing better to do. But mostly, I care about Logan."

I ran my hand across Parrot's fur, who was purring softly next to me on the bed. "I guess that's fair. I hate hurting him like this, but I don't have any other choice."

Alaina scratched Parrot behind the ears. "I'm not blaming you or anything."

"I know."

"So, what do we do now?"

I hopped up from the bed and headed to my closet. "I have some watercolors if you want to mess around with them."

She shrugged like she didn't really care. "Sure. Why not?"

I handed her my set of painting supplies and grabbed my new pencils for myself. Alaina spread herself out on the floor at the foot of my bed while I settled into the purple mushroom chair in the corner of my room. She painted a picture of Parrot while I sketched a portrait of Aaron. We talked about our upcoming senior year and the boys who would be a part of it until my parents came home.

"Want to stay for dinner?" I asked Alaina.

"No, it's okay. My parents probably want me home for supper. I'll see you tomorrow, though."

"Bye." I waved as she exited my room. One last glance at my sketch of Aaron, and my heart melted. I took note of how amazing it was to be able to bring two things I loved together: drawing and Aaron.

After Alaina left, I found my way into the kitchen with my parents. They'd brought us Italian takeout.

"Alaina's not staying for dinner?" my mom asked as she spread the various containers around the table.

"No."

"So, what did you two do all day?" my dad teased when he

entered the kitchen. He leaned against the counter confidently, but he looked ridiculous with his collar popped up in the back. My bet was that he hadn't noticed since removing his tie.

I shrugged. "We painted some pictures for the coven of witches downtown. They needed some more accurate representations of the demons they worship, and we thought we'd lend our services."

My father rolled his eyes. "I'm sure."

I turned from him to keep from laughing and slid into a seat at the table. "Seriously, we just talked and went out for lunch."

"Oh?" my dad asked curiously, following me to the table. "What'd you have?"

"Chicken?" I said it like it was a question. Then I turned to my mother. "By the way, I'm planning lunch with Logan and Aaron again. Is that okay?"

She sighed before pulling her chair out from the table and sitting down. "Maddie, you can't keep leading them both on like that."

"Mom, I know. That's why I want to meet with them."

She eyed me like she didn't quite believe me. "Okay. Can we say grace?"

I contemplated texting Logan and Aaron after dinner, but I wanted to give myself time to sleep on it to make *sure* Aaron was the right choice. Every time I thought about reaching for the phone, my fingers quivered. That didn't help with finishing my sketch of Aaron's perfect features. I fell asleep that night surer than ever that Aaron was the guy I wanted to spend the rest of my life with.

The next morning, I woke after my parents left for work, which was no surprise. I felt no guilt out of milking every moment of sleep I could until school started back up again. I hopped out of bed, feeling even better about my decision this morning than I had after walking out of Chloe's shop yesterday. I poured myself a bowl of cereal and fed Parrot, who was only loving me up to get food. At the table, I texted Aaron and Logan.

Made a decision. Can we meet for lunch?

Logan texted back immediately, and Aaron got back to me a few minutes later. I returned upstairs to get ready for the day. I didn't usually struggle with what to wear, but today, I couldn't seem to decide. I settled on a pair of khaki shorts and a cute purple top after digging through my dresser drawers and closet twice. The doorbell rang just as I finished applying my makeup. I quickly brushed out my hair and then raced downstairs to meet Alaina.

"Hey," she greeted as she entered the house. "Still feeling good about choosing Aaron?"

"I am," I answered confidently.

She took a seat on the couch, and I settled in across from her. We flipped the TV on, but it didn't seem that long before lunchtime arrived. We reached the café a little early, so neither Logan nor Aaron were there. I slid next to Alaina in the booth she'd picked out.

"Ooh." She grabbed for the menu. "Isn't the special today half off pancakes?"

"Hello, ladies. Can I start you off with something to drink?" a waitress named Laura asked.

"I'm fine with water, thanks," I answered.

Alaina gazed up from the menu. "Water is fine with me, too." She looked over at me as soon as Laura left. "You might want to hide that." She pointed to my chest.

I stared down at the angel wing necklace. "Why?"

"Because they'll know right away. Don't you want to wait for both of them to get here?"

"Good idea." I reached up and unclasped the necklace. Not even a moment after I slipped it in my pocket, Aaron entered the café.

He noticed us instantly, and my cheeks flamed at the sight of him. "Hi," he greeted as soon as he was close enough. It was difficult to read his tone.

Laura returned with our waters. "Can I get you anything?" she asked Aaron.

He looked between our drinks. "Sure. Water is fine."

Logan arrived as soon as our waitress set Aaron's drink in front of him.

"Is this everyone?" she asked.

"Yeah," I answered.

"Can I get you anything to drink?" Laura turned to Logan.

I expected him to order a soda like normal, but he didn't want anything. *Smart,* I thought. *He's planning an easy escape.* At least Alaina had come along to comfort him. He'd need it, but at the same time, I didn't regret choosing Aaron.

"Do you need another few minutes with the menu?" Laura asked.

"Yes, please," I told her.

As soon as she left, Aaron spoke. "So, Maddie, who's it going to be?"

"Can't we, uh, eat first?" I looked between the guys but couldn't tell what they were thinking. It's like neither of them knew how to act until I told them who I chose.

"No," Logan said. "I agree with Aaron. I want to know."

I shot Alaina a nervous glance. I could do this. There was no point in dragging it out. "Okay." I cleared my throat. "I choose Aaron."

A grin spread across Aaron's face, displaying his dimple, the same moment Logan's expression fell. At the same time, the tension in my shoulders eased. That was a lot easier than I thought it would be.

"Logan, I'm sorry. We can still be friends." As soon as I said it, I realized that was all we'd ever be now. Friends. And the thing was, I was completely okay with that.

He lifted his gaze to meet mine. "Hey, Maddie. Don't apologize. Whatever makes you happy." I knew he only said it because he cared about me, but his expression told me his heart was breaking. Tears glistened in his eyes, but they were almost unnoticeable.

"Logan," I said. "I mean it. We can still be friends."

"Yeah, Logan." Aaron spoke in a friendly tone. "You'll find someone else. I'm sure of it. You're a great guy."

It amazed me how Aaron could encourage his competition in such a genuine manner. I guess he didn't win a sportsmanship award last year in football for nothing.

"Guys," Logan said sternly. "It's fine. It was a fifty-fifty shot."

I could tell he was only saying that to cheer himself up, but I didn't know what else to do to ease his heartache. "Are you sure you're okay?"

"Yeah, I just..." He stood. "I should probably go."

"No!" I said almost too quickly. "That's not fair." I glanced at Alaina.

"Yeah, Logan," she said. "Stay. Have lunch with me."

I stood. "Aaron and I will go. I'm sorry it had to be this way."

Logan shrugged, but I knew it bothered him.

Aaron took one last sip of his water and then slid out of the booth. "Sorry, man."

I exited the café with Aaron by my side, not once looking back at Logan. As we walked to Aaron's car, I pulled the necklace out of my pocket and clasped it around my neck.

"What now?" he asked.

I wasn't sure. My parents weren't home, so I couldn't take Aaron back there, and I was still hungry. "Can we go find somewhere else to eat?"

"Sure." Aaron pulled out of the parking lot. "You know, I meant it in there."

"Meant what?" My skin grew hot just looking at him. I itched to reach over and grab his hand that rested on the gear shifter between us.

"I meant that he's a good guy. I really do think he'll find someone else. And hey, if you still want to be friends with him, I'm okay with that."

I nodded with a smile and slipped my fingers between his. "Thank you."

In that moment, I knew I'd made the right choice with Aaron.

CHAPTER 5
LOGAN

The next day, I received a text from Alaina saying we were all meeting up for lunch at the café. By "we all," she meant herself, Logan, Jordan, Emily, Holly, Blake, and me. Jordan had returned from his family's last trip up north for the summer, and Alaina was eager to see him. She picked me up on her way there.

I twisted Logan's bracelet around my wrist as we drove. "I didn't tell any of them yet."

"Oh?" she said curiously.

"It seems like everyone's been away all summer except me, you, and Logan. I've hardly texted Emily and Holly all week."

"Me, either, but don't worry. They'll be happy with your choice."

As soon as we entered the café, my heart leapt in my chest. Logan sat beside Jordan and Blake in the corner booth and laughed at something Jordan had said. I wanted to be right there holding his hand and laughing with him.

Alaina tugged at me. Right. I had to actually make my feet move for that to happen.

The boys smiled up at us as soon as we approached. Jordan slid out of his seat and pulled Alaina into a tight embrace. Logan stood and smiled at me, but he didn't move in for a hug. It was like he wasn't sure we were at that point in our relationship yet. I didn't care. I threw my arms around his neck and pulled him close. He could probably feel my heart beating wildly against his body, but if he noticed, he didn't show any indication of it. I grinned so wide it almost hurt my face. I pulled away quickly. Was hugging him okay? I brushed a few stray strands of hair out of my face and slid into the bench next to Blake. Logan sat beside me on the end.

"So, Aaron's out of the picture, then?" Blake asked.

I looked at him. Blake had short brown hair, dark eyes, and deeply tan skin. His eyebrows rose in interest.

"Yep. I—" I glanced at Logan as if searching for the words to explain it. "I'm Logan's girlfriend now."

"Yeah, my man!" Jordan said from across the table. "Congrats."

Logan blushed a deep shade of red, but in the next moment, he composed himself. "Yeah, well, she was worth the wait." He draped his arm across my shoulder, sending my insides melting once again. It made me feel better about hugging him a moment ago, like he welcomed the affection.

"Aww," I heard from across the café. We all looked up to find Emily and Holly approaching our table.

"You two are so cute together." Emily sat, forcing Alaina and Jordan to the middle of the circular booth.

Holly slid in beside her and pushed the dark curls out of her face. "This is great news."

A blush rose to my cheeks again. *Calm yourself, Maddie!* "Yeah, well, we're pretty happy about it."

A moment later, our waitress, Laura, arrived at our table

and took our drink order. After she left, Emily spoke. "Holly and I were thinking about going bowling on Friday. Are you all in?"

"That sounds like fun—" I started to say, but Logan cut me off.

"Actually, I was going to ask you if you wanted to go out on Friday night."

My eyes lit up. Our first date! "Oh. Sorry, guys. I guess we won't make it."

Blake shrugged beside me. "I'm in."

"Yay!" Holly smiled.

"Sorry," Alaina said, "but Jordan and I have a date planned, too."

Emily didn't seem to mind. "That's fine. So, what's everyone's plans for senior year?"

Our drinks arrived, and we ordered our lunch before returning to the conversation. It was nice to have the whole gang together again. It was the first time I remembered all of us being together this summer.

"My plans aren't very fantastic," Holly said. "I have to work if I have any hope of paying for college next year."

"Where'd you get a job?" I asked. "Everywhere I looked wasn't interested."

"My sister got me a job at the restaurant where she waitresses."

"Oh, I didn't know they were hiring."

"They didn't advertise it," Holly told me, "but my sister's a miracle worker. Sorry, but I don't know if I can get you in."

I shrugged. "That's okay. What about you, Emily? What are your plans?"

"Same old, same old." She waved her hand nonchalantly.

"I'm taking choir again and hoping to get better roles in the plays this year."

"Hey." Logan looked at me. "You should join us in choir."

Emily and Logan were the only two in our group who took that elective. It's how they became friends and how Logan slowly eased into our circle.

I glanced between him and Emily. She smiled like she thought it was a good idea.

"Me? In choir?" I raised my brows.

"Why not?" Logan asked. "Then we'd actually share a class together."

"You can sing soprano with me," Emily encouraged. "I've heard you sing before. You're not bad."

I wasn't *terrible*, but I wasn't exactly a performer. Still, I liked the idea of spending as much time with Logan as I could. "I'd have to drop something, and I'm not dropping art. I could maybe drop psychology."

Emily bounced in her chair excitedly.

Logan pulled me even closer to him, sending heat to the surface of my skin. The chatter next to us seemed to fade as he whispered in my ear. "I can't wait to spend more time with you."

The conversation traveled around the table as everyone discussed their plans for the year. Alaina was going to continue her paintings, and she was taking a graphic design class this year to see if it was something she wanted to do for a career. Jordan planned to continue his dancing. Unfortunately, our school didn't offer dance classes, so he took lessons after school at a local studio. He'd spent most of the summer traveling with his dance team when he wasn't on vacation at his parents' cabin. Blake was on the yearbook committee this year. He was a great photographer and had even won money entering his photos in competitions, so the committee was thrilled to have him as their photographer for events.

When our food arrived, everyone broke into their own conversations.

"So, where are you taking me on Friday?" I turned to Logan and bit into my sandwich while he talked.

"Can't it be a surprise?" His lips twitched to hold back a smile, and I found his expression strangely attractive.

"Come on, you can tell me." I moved my hand below the table, intending to grab his for encouragement, but my nerves stalled me. Going from friends to couple was still so new to me. My hand instead curled into a fist and rested on my thigh.

He sighed heavily for show as if I was forcing it out of him and he couldn't help but give in. "Okay. I bought these tickets to *Beauty and the Beast* a while ago. I didn't think it'd be a date when I bought them. I was actually thinking about taking my little brother, but I thought now that we're together, maybe you'd want to go."

"Tickets?"

He nodded. "To the musical. It's at the performing arts center."

"Oh, right. I think Emily mentioned that. It sounds like fun. Are you sure your brother won't be disappointed?"

"Don't worry about it." His fingers slid across mine, and he squeezed my hand.

The butterflies in my stomach sprang to life once again.

I remained mostly silent the rest of the meal. Blake talked loudly beside me between bites of food, but I didn't want to be rude and talk with my mouth full. Apparently he'd missed that lesson as a kid.

"Did you want a ride home?" Alaina asked me after we

finished eating. She licked the last bits of salt off her fingers before wiping them down with the napkin in front of her.

"I'm not sure what my plans are." I exchanged a glance with Logan. "Did you want to hang out?"

"Sure," he agreed.

"Let me just text my parents." I pulled my phone from my purse at my feet and texted my mom. She asked what I'd be doing, if anyone else was going to be around, and all that.

I don't know yet, I texted back.

After a couple of minutes of this, she agreed as long as I didn't take Logan back home when she wasn't there and that if we went to his house, his parents had to be home. Otherwise, she wanted me out in public with him. She also said I had to be home by ten. I nearly rolled my eyes, but I resisted. My friends always joked that my parents were too strict.

I turned back toward Alaina to answer her question. "I'm going to hang out with Logan, so he can drop me off."

"Okay, have fun." She waved as Logan and I stood to go pay our bills.

I squinted into the bright sun as we exited the building. "Have any ideas?"

He wiggled his eyebrows as he unlocked his car. It wasn't the best car in the world. Rust lined the bottom edge, but at least he had a car. "Let's keep this one a surprise, okay?"

I climbed into the passenger seat and reluctantly agreed. Excitement sizzled in my bones. What could he possibly have in store?

My phone buzzed as we drove.

Change your mind yet?

The text was from Aaron. I closed the message app and turned my phone to silent without responding. I didn't want anything to distract me from this moment, from Logan.

Logan drove to the older part of town where Alaina and I went the other day. I breathed a sigh of relief when he stopped before we made it as far as the psychic shop.

"What's this?" I eyed the building in front of us.

"It's a music store."

"Oh. Why are we here?"

We exited the vehicle and headed toward the front door. "It's one of my favorite places," he said, pulling the door open for me.

Cool air hit me when I stepped inside. Guitars hung from the walls, and drum sets stood in one corner. Amps and other accessories filled the additional spaces around the small, crowded room.

"I didn't realize this place existed," I admitted. Each shop on this end of town blended into the next, and new ones came and went so often that I never paid much attention.

"Not a lot of people do," Logan responded.

An older guy with long graying hair and a goatee stepped out from a doorway behind the counter. He was short and thin and hunched over slightly like he'd spent most of his life looking down at something. "Logan," he greeted.

"Hey, Jack."

"I take it you come in here a lot," I teased.

Logan smiled at me then turned to Jack. "Mind if I test her out?"

"Go ahead." Jack smiled.

"Test what out?" I asked.

Logan didn't answer. He simply walked over to one of the acoustic guitars and pulled it down from the wall. Jack drew over a chair for Logan, and he sat down. He patted the guitar. "I call her Lucy."

I giggled. "You named a guitar?"

"Sure did."

Jack returned behind the counter and spoke in a gruff voice. "He's had his eye on that thing ever since it came in a couple weeks ago."

"Jack's been nice enough to steer other customers away from it." Logan winked, making me laugh even harder. "Just another hundred dollars to go, and she's mine." He strummed a chord. "Want to hear her sing?"

I crossed my arms and leaned against the front counter in amusement. "I'd love to."

Logan began fingering notes to a song I didn't recognize. As he sang, his voice filled the room and sent a shiver down my spine. I knew he could sing, but I had no idea he was *that* good. He continued without missing a beat.

What will they say when I'm not around to hear?
Will they call me just a pretty face?
Or will they have better things to say?
What will they say about me when I'm gone?
Will they call me someone?
Or just forget my name?

Well, I don't want to be forgotten.
I want someone to know
that I'm not just a stone.
And I won't be
just measured in square feet.
There's so much more to me,
and I'll let everybody see.

What will they say in ten years down the road?
Will they read the words I left behind?

Or will they be too hard to find?
What will they do when I'm not there to see?
Will they look at pictures of me
or just use them as firewood?

Well, I don't want to be forgotten.
I want someone to know
that I'm not just a stone.
And I won't be
just measured in square feet.
There's so much more to me,
and I'll let everybody see.

Logan sang the chorus one more time before strumming the last few chords. The last chord echoed through the air and hung there for a moment before fading to silence.

It took me several seconds to speak. "Oh my gosh. That song. Those lyrics. They were beautiful."

He quickly turned to hang the guitar back up, but I already noticed his face flaming red. "Thank you."

"Wait, you don't mean…" I glanced at Jack, who was beaming. "Logan, you wrote that?"

He nodded shyly.

"That was amazing! You should get people to pay you for playing."

He shrugged like it wasn't a big deal, but I knew it mattered to him more than that. Music to him was what drawing was to me. "I don't know. It's not really finished yet."

"He's lying," Jack accused lightheartedly. "I hear him come in here almost every day and play that same song. He's good, isn't he?"

I nodded enthusiastically and thought about how lucky I was to have such a talented boyfriend.

~

I greeted Logan at my front door on Friday night. He wore a gray sweatshirt and black pants.

"Hey, we match," I teased. My shirt was darker than his with three-quarter length sleeves, but it was close enough.

He smiled back at me. "You ready?"

"I am." I pushed my way outside and began to shut the door.

"Don't you want me to say hello to your parents or something?" he asked quickly.

I paused and raised my eyebrows. "You want to? They've been teasing me about this date for the past two days. It'd be easier if you didn't."

Logan shrugged like he was unsure. "Okay, I guess."

I adjusted my purse strap on my shoulder and clicked the door shut behind me. A light drizzle sent me running to the passenger side door to keep my hair from getting wet.

Once we were on the road, I spoke again. "Guess what I did yesterday."

"What'd you do?" He glanced at me then back at the road. Small raindrops dotted the asphalt.

I giggled at him. "I said guess."

"You spent the day dreaming about a hunky blond musician?"

I rolled my eyes. "I meant besides that."

He shrugged. "I don't know."

"I went into school and got them to change my schedule. I'm going to be in choir with you now!"

"That's great. Do you think we have any other classes together?"

"I don't have my schedule with me, and I haven't memorized it yet. Changing my elective screwed up my whole schedule. I'm in a different homeroom and everything. I think the only thing that's the same is my art class. We'll have to compare later."

"Too bad Mr. Grady left," Logan said with a fallen face.

"I know," I agreed. "He was the best."

Mr. Grady had been our chemistry teacher last year. He retired at the end of the year, but I think he gave up teaching long before retirement. We spent most days talking amongst ourselves when we were supposed to be doing worksheets. Since Logan and I sat together the second semester, it's what gave me the time to get to know him.

"Remember when our experiment boiled over and Mr. Grady just looked at us and shrugged?" I reminisced.

Logan laughed, and I joined in. "I know. Our senior year is gonna be great." He said it like it was a promise. As long as we were together, I had to agree.

We listened to music on the long drive to the performing arts center in the city. He told me stories from last years' choir performances, and I shared my own tales from art class. It all made me eager to start school again.

We arrived and found our seats. Logan didn't hesitate to slip his fingers into mine and pull me closer to him. I leaned my shoulder into his and could feel the heat radiating off his body. At this point, I hardly cared about the musical. I could sit here the rest of the night simply listening to Logan breathing and still have an amazing time.

"Have you ever seen *Beauty and the Beast*?" he asked.

"You mean besides the Disney version?" I shook my head.

"I think you'll really like it."

People shuffled in from all corners of the arts center, and the vast room buzzed in conversation. I didn't hear my phone vibrate in my purse, but I felt it against the side of my leg.

"Oh, sorry." I bent to retrieve it. "I should probably turn my phone off, huh?"

Logan released my grip, and I checked my screen to find another text from Aaron.

Up to anything fun?

I quickly typed a reply.

Sorry. Busy.

I turned the phone to silent and slid it back into my purse. "Sorry about that."

"Don't worry." Logan draped his arm around me then and pulled me close. My pulse quickened, but in a good way that made me want to melt into him.

The lights dimmed, and the hall fell silent.

"That was a lot better than I expected," I told Logan on the ride home. By now, the sprinkling had stopped, but raindrops had accumulated on the car windows.

"Musicals are fun, aren't they?"

"It actually looked kind of fun to be up there singing," I admitted, not that I'd ever actually *want* to do that. I was content with creating the art rather than *being* it.

"See?" Logan flashed a glance at me before looking back to the road. "It'll be fun to be in choir. You'll like the music."

We listened to the radio the rest of the way home. Logan reached to the controls to turn the music down once he pulled into my driveway. A soft glow filled the car from the front patio light my parents had left on for me.

"It was really fun," I told him, fixing my gaze on his bright blue eyes. "We should do that more often."

His arm came around to rest on the back of my seat. "I'm sure we will."

The air sizzled with electricity between us. My face grew hot while my breaths became shallow. *I should lean in. We both want this.* Neither of us moved for a long time. We simply stared at each other, gauging one another's emotions.

I want this. He wants this. Just do it, Maddie.

I didn't.

Just do it. You have nothing to lose.

My gaze traveled down to his lips. *Do it already, Logan. Kiss me, you fool!*

He slowly leaned in, and I caught my breath a split second before his lips brushed against mine. The whole world stopped in that instant, like this moment was all that existed. And then the moment was over. The hammering of my heart brought me back to reality and reminded me that time was still moving forward.

Logan only pulled away an inch or two.

"Can you do that again?" I whispered. I closed my eyes as his lips touched mine again, and this time, I could feel time moving forward, like this moment would be over far too quickly. My heartbeat pounded throughout my whole body with such force that I wouldn't be surprised if Logan could hear it.

And then he pulled away again. Just like that, it was over.

I tucked a strand of dark hair behind my ear. "I, uh, should probably get inside. My parents are probably wondering what's taking me so long."

He glanced toward the house. "Yeah. I'll see you Monday at school."

"I can't wait." I waved to him as he pulled out of the driveway, and my heart sank at his retreat. I longed to spend just another minute or two with him.

"How'd your date go?" my mom asked from the couch once I entered the house.

"It was great," I told my parents vaguely before racing upstairs and falling down onto my bed with the biggest smile on my face. I replayed the kiss over and over again in my mind, burning it in my memory as I fell asleep that night.

CHAPTER 6

AARON

Aaron invited me out to lunch on Wednesday.

"Where do you want to eat?" he asked when he picked me up.

I knew Jordan would be back from his vacation by now, so I wouldn't be surprised if I ran into him and Logan at our usual café. I didn't think Logan would appreciate seeing Aaron and me together, so I decided to save him the heartache. "Can we try somewhere new? There's that new pizza place on Main Street I haven't tried yet."

"Really? You haven't been there?" Aaron glanced at me. "It's great. You have to try the Hawaiian pizza."

I let out a laugh.

"What?" he asked innocently.

I quieted. "Oh, you weren't joking. I don't like pineapple on my pizza. I'll stick with pepperoni."

"Oh, come on," he encouraged.

A long silence settled over the car while I thought about it. I couldn't resist his smile, so I decided on a compromise. "We'll order half and half, and I'll *try* a piece."

His grin grew wider. "Has anyone told you you're amazing?"

I pressed my lips together to keep from splitting my face open with my smile. "You've mentioned it once or twice."

We arrived shortly and found our way to a booth in the back. Since we already knew what we wanted, it didn't take long to order. I sipped on my water and gazed across the table at Aaron, who was looking down at the napkin he was folding. The rest of the pizzeria seemed to fade away. *I could sit here all day just staring at him and never get bored.*

"Here," he said, pushing the napkin my way.

I finally tore my eyes from his face and noticed his creation for the first time. He'd folded his napkin into a paper crane.

"Wow. That's amazing. The best I can do is one of those fortune teller things."

"The crane is the only thing I ever learned," he laughed.

The rest of our wait consisted of me trying to follow his instructions to make a crane napkin, but by the time our pizza arrived, I still didn't understand what I was doing.

"Forget it." I tossed my napkin aside with a laugh. "Ask me to draw, and I can do that. Ask me to fold paper, and I'm useless."

He grabbed a slice of pepperoni pizza, and I took my bite of his Hawaiian half. Surprisingly, it wasn't that bad.

"See what I told you?" he asked between bites.

I nodded but didn't say anything because my mouth was full. I slowed when I grabbed a slice of pepperoni.

"Excited for school to start next week?" I asked to keep him talking. I loved listening to the sound of his voice.

Aaron swallowed a bite of Hawaiian pizza. "I'm excited for our first game. You'll come, right?"

"Of course. I wouldn't miss it." I bit into my pizza again.

I hadn't attended many football games in the past, but I remembered watching Aaron play tag football in his backyard as a kid during his family's summer barbeques. Of course, my family was always invited on account of our parents being close. The barbeques stopped once our siblings started college and everyone got busy. But I imagined watching a football game would be a lot like that. The times I'd been to school football games, I spent the night eating concession stand food and chatting with my friends. This year, I actually had someone to watch on the field.

Aaron and I talked about sports, art, and school until we were stuffed.

After we finished, he checked his phone for the time. "I still have a little over an hour until football practice."

I didn't want to leave him yet. "Have anything in mind?"

He pressed his lips together. When his eyes met mine, my heart flipped in my chest. "Actually, I do."

He dropped his tip on the table, and we both stood. He was nice enough to pay the bill even though I insisted we split it. We exited the pizzeria hand-in-hand.

"Where are we going?" I asked as I opened the passenger-side door on his car.

Aaron slid into the driver's seat. "To the mall."

I was excited when they decided to build a mall in our town a couple of summers ago, but it ended up being really small and only had a tiny food court and a couple of clothing stores. It wasn't anything exciting, and if you wanted to do any real shopping, you had to head out of town.

"I don't have much money," I admitted.

"Don't worry about it." He smirked as he drove along the street.

I shifted uncomfortably in my seat. I didn't need him buying me anything. He'd just paid for my lunch, and it wasn't fair to ask him for more than that.

Aaron grabbed my hand again once we reached the mall and exited the car. He quickened his pace.

"Where are we going?" I looked up at him, but his expression gave nothing away.

"Just come on. It'll be fun."

"What? What will?" I was still interrogating him as we hurried through the halls of the mall. When he slowed, I finally looked up.

"Come on." He gently pushed me forward. "Get in."

I climbed into the photo booth without question, and he squeezed in beside me. His leg pressed against mine, making me go hot at his touch.

Aaron closed the curtains around us and fed a few dollars into the machine. "Smile."

I did. We started with a smiling pose and finished off with three silly ones. By the time we exited the booth, I was laughing hysterically. I think people were beginning to stare at us.

"What kind of pose was that last one?" I teased between giggles.

"What do you mean? I was being a tiger... or something." He pulled our pictures from the printer and handed me one.

I inspected the last photo. His nose was crinkled up, and his exposed teeth gave the impression that he was growling. It was actually kind of sexy. I tucked the picture in my purse, never wanting to let it go.

"Come on." Aaron grabbed my hand again, dragging me behind him.

"Where are we going now?" The smile never left my face.

"I have another idea." He subtly raised his eyebrows like he had a secret.

We rounded a corner to a dead end, and Aaron pulled me up to a platform in the middle of the hall that had four kiddie rides on it. They were the kind you slip a quarter into and they start swaying and playing music.

I stopped in my tracks. "You're not serious. No."

"Come on, Maddie." He pushed at me. When I didn't budge, he hopped onto the back of a spaceship, gesturing for me to sit in the driver's seat.

I rolled my eyes, reluctantly giving in. If he was willing to do it, then I supposed I had to try as well. I barely fit and had to curl my knees to my chest, but I managed to squeeze myself into the ride.

"Ready?"

Before I could respond, the ride started. I glanced back at him sitting on the surface behind me. "You're going to get in trouble." I pointed over to a sign that said children must stay *inside* the ride at all times.

Aaron scanned the hall, which was mostly empty except for a woman pushing a stroller into one of the nearby shops. The people milling the main hall appeared focused on their destination and didn't seem to notice us.

"Who's going to care? Relax, Maddie."

His arm stretched out in front of me, and before I knew it, he snapped a couple of selfies while I threw my head back in laughter. I couldn't stop when I was around him.

My heart nearly broke when he dropped me off at home afterward so he could go to football practice. We stood on my front steps, and I wrapped my arms around him, resting my head on his chest. I could feel his hot breath on the top of my head.

"I don't want you to leave," I whispered. "I want to spend more time with you."

He hugged me back. "I know. I want to spend more time with you, too. You don't want to come watch me practice, do you?"

I didn't answer while I contemplated the idea. It would be nice to be around him more, but it's not like I'd actually be *with* him while he was practicing. Then again, it'd be a lot like attending his games, and I'd rather do that than hang out at home without him. *Will Mom and Dad let me go?*

"Hey." Aaron pulled away from me like he just had a great idea. "I just thought of something. Why don't you join cheer-leading?"

I drew away another few inches to look him in the eyes. "Cheerleading? Aaron, I'm not—"

"Yeah," he interrupted like it was the best idea ever. "Then you could watch me every game. I could drive you to and from practice."

I liked the idea of being near him, but I wasn't cheer-leading material. "Aaron, I'm not a cheerleader. I don't do cartwheels and back handsprings and stuff like that. Besides, didn't they already start practicing?"

"Yeah, but Dani told us last week that they were looking for more girls. We're talking sideline cheerleading, Maddie. You don't need to know how to do a back handspring."

I let the idea sink in. Our school wasn't big enough for a competitive cheer squad, so most people avoided the sport because it wasn't "cool" enough for them. Other girls joined cross country, swimming, or volleyball, or there were people like me who never cared to join a sport at all.

"I don't know, Aaron," I told him, but I had to admit, the idea intrigued me.

"Just check out their practice," he pleaded. "It's not as tough as you probably think it is. Sure, they do pyramids and cartwheels, but not all the girls do flips and stuff. They said they needed some more people for their stunts. I think you'd like it."

If it meant spending more time with him, I probably would enjoy it. I shrugged. "I guess I could give it a shot."

"Awesome. Do you want to change? I can give Dani a call and see if it's okay if you join practice."

"Okay." I rushed upstairs and quickly changed into my royal blue Soffe shorts and a white t-shirt, our school colors. I brushed my hair into a ponytail and laced my shoes. My hands shook the whole time. Was I actually excited about the idea of being a *cheerleader*?

No, I told myself. I was just happy to have more time with Aaron.

"Good news," Aaron smiled when I made it back downstairs. "Dani says they'd love to see what you can do. Practice starts soon, so we better get going."

I texted my mom in the car, telling her where I was going. She told me to have fun and cheer really loud. I wasn't sure if she was making fun of me or actually encouraging me. She was probably happy I was trying some extracurricular. I supposed it was time to try something besides art while I had plenty of opportunities at my fingertips. *But cheerleading?* I wondered. Then I quickly reminded myself that if this worked out, it meant I'd have more time with Aaron. And that made the nerves seem worth it.

I stepped out of Aaron's car nervously when we made it to the football field. The warm air and shining sun were pleasant on my exposed skin. I glanced toward Aaron. "Are you sure they want me to join? I missed tryouts."

"Maddie, there weren't enough girls at tryouts to *have* tryouts."

I squinted across the vast clearing at the girls stretching in a grassy area outside the boundaries of the field. "You're sure?"

"Do you want me to go with you?" His voice was soft and reassuring.

I knew he had to go change for his practice, but I nodded anyway.

He shook his head at me but couldn't hide his amused smile. "Dani," Aaron called as soon as we were close enough.

Dani hopped up from the ground where she was stretching. Her brown ponytail swished from side to side as she raced up to us. "Maddie." She had sweet eyes and a friendly smile. I knew her from several classes we'd had together, but I hadn't talked to her much. "You're a lifesaver!"

I didn't know what to say or do, so I simply let Dani drag me away. I waved back at Aaron as he retreated to attend his own practice.

"Coach," Dani called to a woman who looked to be about forty.

I'd never met their coach before. She had a short brown pixie cut with blond highlights, and her smile stretched across her entire face.

"This is Maddie," Dani introduced. "She's interested in joining the team."

"Hi, Maddie," she greeted. "I'm Nikki. You can call me Nikki or Coach, whichever you prefer."

All I could do was give her a friendly smile.

Coach pressed her lips together. "Hmm... Let me think about how I want to do this. We need the extra girls, but I can't guarantee you a spot on the team until we know what you can do."

Dani cut in. "Last week you had me teach Rachel some cheers while everyone else practiced."

Coach thought about it for a few seconds longer. "I know. I just don't want to take more time out of practice than we need to."

Dani shrugged. "I know all the cheers anyway."

"I wanted to work on some stunts today, too," Coach said. "Okay, here's what we'll do. We'll all warm up together, and then you can teach Maddie some cheers while we go through the school song. When we take our break, I'll see what Maddie can do, and if she's okay to join the team, she can stay and watch us work on stunts. Sorry, Maddie, but I'll need you to sign a waiver and some medical forms before you can join everyone for stunts."

I didn't say a thing the whole time.

"Sounds good," Dani agreed. "Come on, Maddie." She led me to an open spot on the grass to stretch. "Don't worry about making the team. We needed another person for one of the stunts anyway. Just keep your arms straight, yell loud, and clap on the beat. Coach will love you."

"Thanks," I told Dani, but it came out more like a whisper.

I still wasn't sure about this whole cheerleading thing, and Dani almost seemed too bubbly and nice for her own good. Was she being nice because she actually thought I'd fit in here, or was it because I was dating Aaron? That had to put me a notch higher on the "cool" scale, right? Or maybe Dani was just naturally kind. Considering the cheerleaders at our school didn't fit the stereotypical "mean girl" formula, it was probably because she was just that nice.

When I looked up and spotted Aaron across the field, my

anxiety eased. In that moment, I convinced myself that maybe I actually had what it took, that maybe I'd actually enjoy myself.

An hour later, I'd learned three cheers, the first half of the school song, and that I could actually do a decent cartwheel. When Coach called for a break, my hands broke into a nervous sweat.

Apparently Dani noticed. "Don't worry. You'll do great. Remember to keep those arms straight."

I gave a shy smile. "Thanks."

"Let's see what you can do," Coach said.

Dani ran through the cheers with me the first time, but she sat out the second time so I could try them on my own. Luckily, none of the other girls paid attention.

Arms straight. Yell loud. Clap on the beat. Why am I doing this again? I glanced toward the field to remind myself and suddenly felt a surge of confidence. *I can do this.*

"Be aggressive," I started. I focused on remembering the motions Dani had taught me and to keep my arms straight.

When I finished all three cheers, Coach gave me that wide smile again. "Great form, Maddie. You have a lot to learn, but welcome to the team."

I sat out the rest of practice and watched the girls do stunts that thankfully didn't look overly complicated. I returned home that night exhausted, my head swimming with new information.

"Did you make the team?" my mother called from the kitchen.

I joined her and my father at the table, where they were already eating dinner without me. "I did."

"That's great," my mom said with a smile.

"Congratulations," my dad told me. "I just hope this doesn't mean you'll let your grades slip."

I sighed. "I won't, Dad."

"Or your art," he warned with a full mouth.

"Please, Dad. Nothing could make me slack on my art. I just thought getting involved in something new might get me out of the house." I shrugged like it was no big deal.

My father laughed. "Of all the things that could get you out of the house, I never would have thought cheerleading would be one of them."

I raised a challenging eyebrow and bit back in an equally playful manner. "Of all the people who would make fun of me for it, I never would have thought the first would be my own father."

"Settle down, children," my mother said, glaring at my dad.

He gazed back innocently.

I turned to my mom, serious this time. "I need you to sign some stuff before tomorrow's practice. Coach said something about me needing a physical, too."

My mother swallowed the food in her mouth. "I'll call Dr. Thalis tomorrow and see if she can work you in to her schedule. We helped her sell her house last month, and I know she'd be happy to do us a favor."

"Thanks, Mom."

I spent the next two days practicing my cheers and learning how to spot the flyers. At least I didn't have to go up in the air. By Friday night, I was mentally exhausted. Aaron dropped me off at home and said he'd be back in an hour to pick me up for our date after we both had a chance to shower.

"How was practice?" my father asked from the couch when I walked in the door. He didn't look up from his laptop he was working on. I could hear my mother moving around the kitchen, probably cleaning up after the supper I'd missed.

"It was good. I learned some new cheers today. Dani says I'm doing pretty good."

"Invite her over sometime, will you? I want to meet this new friend of yours." He finally turned around to face me.

"I will. By the way, it's okay if I go out with Aaron tonight, right?" I knew he didn't mind. My parents were already in love with him and had been teasing me non-stop about how they always figured we'd end up together. They were also full of it.

"As long as you're home by eleven. What are you two going to do?"

I left a peck on my father's cheek. "Thanks, Dad. We're going bowling."

"That should be fun," he called after me as I raced up the stairs.

I showered and blow dried my hair before dressing in my casual jeans and tee. I applied a layer of eyeshadow, liner, and mascara with a touch of lip gloss. I finished off my ensemble with Aaron's angel wing pendant.

While waiting, I checked my phone on my desk. Still no text from Logan. I'd tried to contact him over the last few days to make sure he was all right, but he never wanted to talk. He always said he was busy. Alaina told me he was doing fine, but I didn't believe either one of them.

"There's my angel," Aaron greeted when I opened the door to him. He took a step into the house to say hello to my parents.

My father finally stood and rounded the couch to shake

Aaron's hand. "Have her home by eleven, okay?"

"Yes, Mr. Rose."

My mother emerged from the kitchen then and exchanged a few pleasantries with him, asking how his parents were and all of that. After a few minutes that seemed to drag, my parents finally let us go.

"Sorry about that," I told Aaron once we reached the car.

He glanced toward the house. "About what? Your parents? Don't worry about it. I like them."

It wasn't long before we pulled up in front of the bowling alley. A light drizzle left splats of small raindrops on the windshield.

"You know I'm not very good at bowling, right?" I admitted.

Aaron shrugged. "That's why I invited you. I have to win against someone." A smirk formed across his face.

"Hey," I scolded playfully.

We entered the bowling alley and started by ordering burgers and fries. The place was busy since it was the Friday before school started and it was one of the only things to do in town. Everyone was trying to get in one last good night before the summer ended.

I dipped my fry into my mound of ketchup and noticed Aaron was eating his plain. "You don't like ketchup?" I asked in surprise.

He crinkled his nose. "Not really." He reached for the mustard and squeezed some next to his fries.

"Ew! You don't like ketchup, but you'll douse your fries in mustard? What's wrong with you?"

He shrugged. "I'm dating you."

I had the urge to throw a fry at him but resisted. Instead, I just laughed. I quieted the moment I noticed a group of teens my age walk through the front doors.

Aaron turned to follow my gaze and spoke quietly. "I'm sorry. I didn't know they'd be here."

"It's okay."

I shifted uncomfortably in my seat when Logan noticed me watching him. He quickly averted his gaze. Emily and Holly waved to me when they saw me, but they could see I was on a date and didn't come over to bother me.

"I just feel bad about Logan," I admitted. "I tried telling him I was sorry, but he won't take my texts."

"Hey, Maddie," Aaron said softly. "It's not your fault how he feels."

"I know." I shook off a shudder. "I can't help feeling that it is, though."

"If he doesn't want to be friends with you anymore, it's his loss."

I finally looked Aaron in the eyes, and it didn't take much for me to agree with him. "You're right. His loss."

Aaron and I pulled on our rental shoes and headed to our lane. Neither of us was surprised when he won by a long shot. It didn't matter, though, because I had more fun watching him perform his "lucky dance" before every shot he took. I was still laughing by the time we exited the bowling alley.

"I don't have to be home for a couple of hours yet," I told him. "Did you have anything else in mind?"

He thought about it for a moment. "Let's go back to my house. We can watch a movie."

I greeted his parents when we walked in the house. They both sat in front of the TV, but it was like they could sense our intentions and quickly abandoned the living room. His father escaped to their bedroom to turn on his show in there, and his mother announced she was going to bake cookies in the kitchen. She was probably trying to give us privacy while still being able to hear what was going on.

I sat on the couch and looked around nervously. I'd been in the Harding's house plenty of times over the years, but it seemed different this time. The familiar scent of fresh laundry filled the house, but the photos on the walls seemed brighter and more vibrant. When Aaron situated himself next to me and wrapped his arm around my shoulder, I realized what was different about it all. I wasn't just in the Harding's house anymore. I was in my boyfriend's house, sitting on my *boyfriend's* couch, in his arms.

Aaron flipped through Netflix until we found a movie we both agreed on. By twenty minutes in, I was already starting to drift off.

"Is it boring you that much?" The sound of Aaron's voice jolted me awake. Honestly, I didn't care that much about the movie. I was simply enjoying being in his arms.

"I'm sorry. No, it's just…"

"It's okay. It's really not a good movie. I have another idea." He stood and headed down the hall, leaving me to wonder what he could possibly have in mind. He came back a few moments later with a pile of sheets in his arms.

"What are those for?"

He flipped the TV off. "A fort, of course."

A smile spread across my face.

We spent the next half hour stretching his family's sheets across the living room. When we were finally done, we stood back to admire our work.

"Just like when we were kids," I pointed out.

He bounced on the balls of his feet. "Ready to see the inside?" He parted the sheets, and I crawled inside.

The top of our fort grazed against my head. "It definitely feels smaller than when we were kids."

"Well, we'll have to adjust, then."

I eyed the top of the fort, wondering how we could raise the ceiling. "Well, we could—"

I never had a chance to finish because in the next moment, Aaron wrapped his arms around my body and pulled me back until we were lying on the living room floor looking up at the ceiling of our fort. A soft blue hue filled the space as the light filtered in through the sky blue sheets above us.

"See?" Aaron asked. "We still fit."

I melted into him, letting my head rest in a comfortable position on his chest. The arm he'd wrapped around me was comforting and warm, and he pulled me even closer to him. Neither of us said a word as we locked our eyes on one another. I barely noticed the fresh scent of cookies wafting through the air or the hum of the desktop in the corner of the room. All that mattered was him—was us—as we stared into each other's faces for what could have been minutes or a lifetime. There was no way of gauging the time.

Eventually, his voice cut through the silence. "Who would have guessed that we'd end up here?"

I smiled up at him. "I know. Years ago we were building these forts and eating popcorn under them while watching movies with my sisters and your brother. Now it's just you and me."

Before I knew what was happening, Aaron shifted until he hovered over me, his face just inches from my own. He raised his eyebrows and repeated my last words in just a whisper. "Just you and me."

I felt his sweet breath on my face when he talked, and my lips quivered in response. I didn't even have a moment to think about what was coming next before he swiftly closed the distance between us and pressed his lips to mine. My entire body came alive in that moment, sending adrenaline coursing through my veins. The surface of my skin warmed, and my heart hammered against my rib cage. He kissed me again and again, never once pulling away. I locked my hands on the side of his face, begging him to never stop.

"Aaron," his mother called.

My heart leapt in my chest, and he pulled away from me at record speed. When I realized there was no way she witnessed our make out session, I relaxed.

"Yeah?" he called back.

"It's getting late. You should probably take Maddie home."

He sighed. "Sorry."

My face fell in disappointment. "I wish this night didn't have to end."

"Don't worry." He touched a finger to my cheek and stared down into my eyes again. "We'll have many more nights like this one. I promise."

I returned home wanting nothing more than a few more moments alone with him, but his words brought me comfort as I crawled into bed that night and fell asleep dreaming of him.

CHAPTER 7
LOGAN

I woke early on the first day of school, eager to get back into the routine of hanging out with my friends and attending art class. I wasn't sure what to expect from choir, but at least Logan and Emily would be there. I dressed in my new first day of school outfit my mom bought me a couple of weeks ago: a new pair of dark jeans with a mauve cardigan over a white lace tee. To finish off my first day of school look, I pulled my hair into a decent messy bun. I ate breakfast and tightened Logan's bracelet around my wrist before leaving for school.

The school wasn't far, which was good for me since I didn't have a car, so I pulled my bike from the garage and pedaled to school. I met up with my friends near our lockers. I had the same locker as last year but had to memorize a new combination. Logan pulled me into a hug. I wanted so badly to press my lips to his, but we both resisted since teachers and other students were milling nearby.

"What's up?" I drew away from Logan to look him in the eyes.

"We're all comparing our final schedules."

I pulled mine from my pocket and unfolded it, turning to the rest of the group. I still hadn't memorized the changes since I'd added choir as an elective. I ended up having at least one class with all my friends, and Logan and I even shared homeroom together. That meant we'd see each other for first period, lunch, and our last hour choir class. Alaina and I were in math and art together, and the rest of my friends had a class with me here and there.

The warning bell rang shortly after, and I abandoned my friends to drop my bag in my locker. When I swung it shut and looked up, I spotted Aaron crouched by his locker at the other end of the hall. His eyes caught mine, and I quickly looked away. Most of the other students had already fled the halls to their homerooms, so there weren't many people left at their lockers. I passed by Aaron on my way to my first class, not bothering to look at him.

"Maddie," he called before I made it out of ear shot.

I paused and held in the sigh I urged to let out. I knew what he was going to say, and I wasn't interested in hearing how wrong I was to choose Logan. I turned to him. He stood and shut his locker but didn't advanced toward me.

"Aaron, I—"

"How've you been?" He shifted his weight between his feet while the last few students trickled into their classrooms.

"I've been fine, but I should get to class. You're okay, right?"

He stared down at the floor for a moment before looking at me. An attempt at a smile masked his true emotions. "Yeah, I'm fine."

I didn't know how to respond, so I spit out the first thing I could think of. "By the way, did you want your necklace back?"

"No," he answered almost too quickly. "Keep it. That way you can think of me."

I couldn't find the words to reply.

Luckily, Aaron spoke first. "Well, uh, gotta get to class. See you later."

"Bye, Aaron." I hurried off in the opposite direction and slipped into my first hour class just as the final bell rang. An open seat next to Logan in the front welcomed me, and I settled in beside him.

At lunch, I found my way to my friends at our table. "Hey," I greeted Blake, Emily, and Holly. Jordan, Alaina, and Logan showed up shortly after me. Logan settled in on my left while Alaina sat to my right across from Jordan in the same seats we sat in last year. I slid my hand into Logan's under the table, hoping none of the teachers would notice.

"Have any ideas for homecoming yet?" Holly asked me from across the table.

I glanced up from my chicken. "Homecoming? When is that again?"

"Isn't it early this year?" Alaina asked. "I thought it was in about four weeks, right? Normally it's the last game of the season, but most of the games later in the season are away games."

Holly nodded. "Right. Emily and I were talking and thought maybe we should be thinking about dress shopping."

Dress shopping. Add that to the list of things I had to ask my parents money for. But I wasn't going to sit at home like I did last year. This year, I actually had a date, and it was my last chance to attend the homecoming dance.

"I think getting together for dress shopping would be fun," I told her.

Emily sighed. "I'm busy the next two weekends, so we'd have to go the week before the dance. That's not too late to do it, is it?"

Alaina shrugged. "I don't think so. We don't need more than one day to look, do we?"

None of us were exactly fashionistas, but I *did* want to look nice for Logan. "I think one day will be fine if we hit up the mall and those other two stores over on that end of town. Or maybe we could head out of town."

"Okay," Alaina agreed. "Let's meet up in the food court at the mall that Saturday morning, say around ten?"

We all agreed that sounded great.

"Hey," Jordan cut in. "Did any of you meet the new science teacher yet?"

The conversation quickly shifted to our new classes and teachers. I tuned out the discussion and turned to Logan.

"You okay?" I asked.

He swallowed his food before speaking. "Me? I'm fine. Why?"

"You've been quiet all through lunch."

He gave my hand a light squeeze. "I'm just running some lyrics through my head and slightly dreading my calculus class I have next period."

"Don't worry about it. You'll do great." I tightened my grip on his hand for encouragement. "You know, I've heard that people who are good at music are also good at math. Something about how music theory is really all about mathematical equations."

Logan let out a light laugh. "Yeah, I'm sure I'll do fine."

~

Alaina and I walked together to art class. It was advanced 2D art, mostly focusing on paintings and drawings, which made it perfect for Alaina and me. Sadly, we didn't get to do any art the first day because it was all about going through the syllabus and learning how the class would work for the semester.

"This landscape painting project should be fun." Alaina pointed to the syllabus.

"I'm looking forward to the weekly sketches we have to do," I told her.

She wrinkled her nose. "Think I can just paint in my sketchbook instead?"

"Probably not."

By the time the last hour of the day—choir—rolled around, I was sick of skimming through syllabi and reviewing classroom rules, but when I walked into the music room and spotted Logan, my mood lifted.

"Maddie," Emily called, waving me over and gesturing to a chair between her and Logan.

"Hi." I gave an uncertain smile.

"This is the soprano section," Emily explained. "The tenors and bases sit in the middle, and the altos sit over there." She pointed to the other side of the semi-circle of chairs.

"Well, that's good. Then I can sit by both of you."

Logan smiled beside me. "You're going to have a lot of fun. I'm sure of it."

The room fell silent as soon as the bell rang. We spent the hour reviewing the syllabus and organizing our folders for our music. Our director, Mr. Banks, handed out a couple of booklets with music and lyrics written inside, and we took the last few minutes of class to sight read one of them. I didn't know a lot about music and had a hard time keeping up with the notes, but it wasn't as difficult the second time through since I'd already heard it once. Logan's tenor voice beside me filled me with warmth.

Mr. Banks announced that the rest of the week he would be testing each student for their vocal range, and I only hoped I'd stay in the soprano section so I could sit by Emily and Logan.

By Friday night, I had eased back into the swing of the school year. I spent the afternoon relaxing on my back porch and working on homework before flipping my sketchbook open and drawing an image for art class. I stared out at the flowers in the backyard for several minutes, wondering what I should draw. Would it be weird if I sketched another image of Logan's face for my teacher to see? When my eyes drifted back to my hand, I knew what to sketch.

When my parents arrived home, I closed my sketchbook and slipped Logan's bracelet back on my wrist. I was proud of the sketch I'd drawn of it since I managed to capture the texture of each strand.

"You hungry, Maddie?" my dad asked when I stepped into the kitchen. "Mom's warming up some soup."

"Yeah, I could use some food." I leaned against the counter while I spoke. "Logan is picking me up soon, though, so I should be quick."

My mother turned from the cupboard with three bowls in her hand. "Where are you headed with him again?"

"Well, Logan has to play in the pep band for the football game tonight. Then we thought maybe we'd hang out."

"Okay," my mom said. "You know your Friday curfew. Be home by eleven."

When the doorbell rang, I hopped up from the table to get it, but my dad was faster than me.

"Dad, what are you doing?"

He looked back with a teasing smile. "I want to meet this guy."

"Dad." I stopped him just as his fingers grazed the door knob. "Try not to embarrass me, okay?"

"I won't," he assured with an eye roll before opening the door and welcoming Logan inside.

Logan cleared his throat. "Uh, hello sir, uh, Mr. Rose, uh…"

"Call me Will," he said, shaking Logan's hand firmly.

I stood behind my father, praying he wouldn't say much else.

My mother had followed behind me and stuck her hand toward Logan, too. "I'm Evelyn. Nice to meet you." The look she gave me added the word she didn't say out loud. *Finally.*

I grabbed my purse and hoodie from the couch, pushed past my parents before they could say anything else, and slid my arm into the crook of Logan's elbow. "Well, we better be going. Don't want Logan to be late for warm-ups. Bye!"

"Have fun," my mom called the same time my dad said, "Don't be home too late."

"I'm sorry," I told Logan in the car. "My parents are…" I shrugged when I couldn't find the right words.

Logan glanced at me as he drove. "There's nothing wrong with your parents. They love you is all."

"Yeah, I know they do."

It didn't take long to reach the football field. Logan lugged his saxophone case out of the back of his car and opened it to assemble his instrument.

I crossed my arms over my chest and leaned against the side of his car. "So, is playing in the pep band any fun?"

It took a moment for Logan to answer since he had a reed in his mouth. "It's a lot of fun. The songs are more upbeat than in concert band, and you get free admission to any events where the band plays."

I'd never really been one for attending school functions. "So, are you guys any good?"

Logan let out an amused laugh and stood up straight. His assembled saxophone hung around his neck. "We're okay, but the freshmen are still learning the songs."

I took his hand in mine. "Well, I finally get to hear you play."

"Keep your distance," he warned with a warm smile that quickened my heart rate. "It's going to get intense."

I didn't quite believe him until I was sitting in the stands next to him during their pre-game performance. It wasn't just that the music was loud, but the band put a lot of movement to the music. Some of them—including Logan—even mildly danced to it.

While they played, I spotted Aaron on the field warming up. His eyes scanned the bleachers until they fell on me. For a split second, I thought that maybe he was just looking at the band, but somehow, I could feel his eyes on me. I gave him a shy wave to acknowledge him, hoping it was friendly enough to show I didn't want to completely write him off from my life. I really did want to try being friends with him—as long as he was no longer interested in getting me to change my mind about Logan.

By the time the band finished playing their fifth or sixth song, Logan was laughing with his buddies. I couldn't help but giggle along, simply because I enjoyed seeing him so happy. The band settled down a few minutes before the start of the game. They all turned to a new sheet of music, and I watched as the small team of cheerleaders assembled themselves in a formation on the sidelines. A new tune broke out from the band, and I recognized it as our school song. The cheerleaders danced along with a simple routine and ended in what looked to be an even easier stunt. To be fair, it didn't look like they had enough girls to do much more than an elevator and a thigh stand.

I spoke quietly to Logan as announcements rang out over the loudspeaker. "Was that it? Are you done playing?"

He slid closer to me, the side of my body growing hot at each point he touched it. "No," he whispered back in an equally quiet voice. His thumb ran along the backside of my hand he was holding. "We still have to play the national anthem. Then we have to play during half time. We can leave after that if you want, or we can stick around and watch the rest of the game."

"We'll see," I answered.

I stood and placed my hand over my heart when the Star Spangled Banner played. I could have sworn that for a second Aaron looked my way again from his position on the field, but by the time I could really process his moving eyes, they had already passed me.

When the national anthem ended, I sat and nestled close to Logan for the first half of the game, not really paying attention to what was happening on the field. Instead, I focused on the warmth of Logan's leg against my own. His touch was so comforting that I barely noticed the chilly night air between us. I ran my thumb over the rough callouses at the ends of his fingers, earned from his years of guitar playing.

People cheered all around me, but even when I was watching the game, I wasn't really seeing what was going on. That is, until Aaron prepared to kick a field goal. I held my breath for him, wishing him luck. His eyes scanned the bleachers one last time, finding me in them. I didn't know what else to do but give him a thumbs up in encouragement. I slowly let out a breath as the ball sailed through the air, but my wishing did no good. He missed the field goal.

"Dang," Logan said, but I didn't spot any sincerity in his comment.

Aaron's shoulders slumped as he returned to the sidelines. I had the sudden urge to comfort him once I had the chance. *You can't, Maddie. You're not his girlfriend,* I reminded myself. At this point, I wasn't even sure we were friends.

"So, do you want to stay and finish watching the game or head out?" Logan asked at the end of half time.

I gazed out onto the field at Aaron. He was the only thing besides Logan keeping me here, and honestly, Aaron didn't really need me.

I turned to Logan and put a smile on my face. "Let's go."

We had enough time for a movie, and luckily there was a decent one playing at the dollar theatre shortly after we arrived.

"Want popcorn or anything?" Logan asked.

"I guess so," I answered, diving into my purse to pull out the few dollars I had.

"Don't worry about it. I can get it."

I shifted uncomfortably at the snack counter. I didn't have a job and therefore didn't have much money, but I didn't like the idea of Logan paying for everything. Then again, he *was* my boyfriend, and that was the typical way things went. I knew he had some money he made from tutoring some middle school kids, but since he hadn't tutored much over the summer, I wondered how much he had. I didn't want him to drain his savings for me, especially when he was saving up for his guitar.

"Logan," I pulled at him before he had a chance to reach the counter. "I don't need any popcorn. I had dinner, so I'm not very hungry."

He shrugged. "I'll get two for me, then. If a bag of popcorn happens into your lap, it wasn't my fault."

I smiled back at him, appreciative of his kind gesture. With no one around who would scold us, I pulled him into a hug and planted a kiss on his lips right there.

CHAPTER 8

AARON

I woke up the first day of school mildly excited, not so much for classes, but because I enjoyed the time I could spend with my friends. I was also eager to get back to my art classes that I'd missed so much throughout the summer. I rode my bike to school and found Aaron at his locker. My friends gathered nearby comparing their class schedules. I still wasn't sure if Logan would be comfortable with me around, so I waved and smiled but mostly steered clear.

"There's my angel," Aaron said in a low voice when I approached. He closed his locker and leaned against it, brushing a strand of dark hair out of my eyes. "How was your weekend?"

I smiled up at him. "Filled with a lot of practicing cheers in my backyard. Thank goodness I have a fence so I didn't freak out the neighbors. They probably would have thought I was having a seizure otherwise."

Aaron stared down at his fingers and grazed them across mine. "Oh, come on. You can't be that bad."

I laughed. "Well, they let me on the team, so I guess I'm not."

He looked back up at me. "How'd you get to school? Did you walk?"

"I rode my bike. Why?"

Aaron licked his lower lip and stared into my eyes like I was the only girl in the world. "Leave it at home tomorrow. I'll pick you up. Besides, I said I'd drive you home from practice. How can I do that when you have to get your bike back home?"

More time with Aaron? Sign me up!

"That sounds like a fantastic idea." I leaned into him as if magnetized. At the same time, I noticed my group of friends separate and head to their homerooms. "Give me a sec, will you?" I quickly caught up with Alaina and called her name.

She turned to me with a smile.

"Hey, how's Logan?" I asked. "Better?"

Her stick-straight hair bobbed over her shoulder when she nodded. "Yeah, he's fine."

I breathed a sigh of relief. "Good. He still won't answer my texts, though. It won't be weird if we sit together at lunch?"

"No, Maddie." Alaina twisted her face into an expression that said I was being ridiculous. "It'll be like old times. We're all still friends, whether you and Logan are a thing or not. Don't worry about it. He'll be able to handle it."

"Okay," I said uncertainly. "I'll see you in art."

She waved. "See ya."

"Sorry about that," I told Aaron once I returned.

"No problem." He clicked his locker shut and followed me to mine.

"What's your schedule like?" I asked as I double checked my combination on my class schedule. After twisting in the numbers, I hung my bag inside and quickly pulled out a notebook and pencil for first period.

"I have Saunders first period and…" He paused to pull his schedule from his pocket. "And then I have math, English…"

I glanced at the paper in his hands. "Oh, I think we're together for English. Other than that, I don't think we have any classes together. You didn't happen to enroll in 2D art, did you?"

The look on his face told me he wouldn't be caught dead taking an art class.

"I'm kidding, Aaron. I'll see you in English." I almost leaned in to kiss him goodbye before realizing we were in school where PDA wasn't tolerated. Instead, I simply waved while I retreated from him. It almost felt like a little piece of my heart stayed with him as he walked in the opposite direction. I reached to my chest to feel his necklace, and I knew that at the very least, a piece of him stayed with me.

In English, Aaron and I found a spot together near the back of the class. I noticed Dani from across the room. She caught my eye and waved at me, and I smiled back. It was nice to be welcomed so quickly into her circle. Turns out she was super nice to everyone, so it no longer felt strange that she'd been so nice to me my first day of practice.

"Another year with Mrs. Gates." Aaron pulled my attention back to him and wiggled his eyebrows at me. "This should be fun."

It was no secret that most students weren't a big fan of Mrs. Gates because she gave out a lot of homework, but I rather enjoyed her writing assignments.

"Can't handle a little creative writing homework?" I teased, scooting my chair an inch closer to him. I still felt too far away.

The bell rang, and a silence settled over the room. Mrs. Gates went over the normal first day routine by handing out our syllabus and getting us settled into assigned seats near members of our first project group. I hated assigned seats and randomly selected groups because it meant Aaron and I wouldn't be sitting next to each other, though that was probably a good thing. I doubt I'd be able to concentrate on schoolwork with his dimpled smile distracting me every two seconds. At the very least, Mrs. Gates had assigned Dani and me to the same group, so we ended up sitting next to each other. Still, I found my gaze constantly drifting across the room to the back of Aaron's head. I wished we'd been assigned to the same group.

"Having English class together does us no good if we don't get to sit by each other," I complained to him in the lunch line later that day.

He shrugged. "I know. It sucks. But it's not like we're stuck in these groups for the whole semester. It's just a couple weeks, and then we get new groups. We might end up next to each other eventually." His optimism helped melt my disappointment.

Aaron tore his eyes off me and smiled toward some of his friends seated at a table across the cafeteria. And that's when it hit me. We were going to have to choose between my table and his. I hadn't even considered how he'd feel about sitting with my group of friends.

"Aaron," I asked with uncertainty, "where are we going to sit?"

His gaze flickered between his table and mine. "Oh, uh, I

thought we'd sit at my table. I mean, Logan still isn't taking your texts, is he?"

I inched to the front of the cafeteria as the line moved. "No, he's not. Alaina says he's fine, but I'm not sure he actually still wants to be friends."

"Hey, my friends are going to love you." His touched my fingers lightly, sending a surge of electricity throughout my body. "I promise."

I gave my friends a smile as we passed by their table with our trays. The girls all waved back with a look in their eyes that said they understood my choice, but none of the guys seemed to notice. Aaron's table was filled with a couple of football players and their girlfriends. Luckily, I knew one girl well enough that I didn't feel completely out of my element. I slid into a seat beside Dani, who was dating Aaron's friend, Brandon. She was the only other cheerleader at the table.

Conversations broke into small groups of two or three. I held onto Aaron's hand under the table but spent most of my time talking to Dani about cheers, stunts, and her ideas for the team apparel we were going to order this year. She wanted to know my opinion on whether we should get t-shirts or hoodies, sweat pants or shorts, or all of them. I voted for the hoodies. As I was dumping my tray, I realized what it meant for Dani to consider my opinion. For the first time since I met the cheerleaders on the football field, I really felt like a part of the team.

In art class, I finally had a chance to talk to Alaina. "Hey, you don't think anyone is mad at me for sitting with Aaron at lunch, do you?"

She shrugged and spoke in a soft voice, her eyes locked on the pencil she was twirling around in her fingers. "I understand. He's your boyfriend now. You know there's always a spot open for you at our table, though, right? And for Aaron."

"Maybe we could trade off which table we sit at."

"Yeah, you missed out on the conversation today."

My heart broke a little, leaving me feeling left out. "Oh? Was it interesting?"

She wrinkled her nose and shook her head. "Not really, but Emily, Holly, and I talked about going dress shopping the week before homecoming. Are you in?"

"That's right. Homecoming is early this year." I couldn't help but picture Aaron and me dancing together in the decorated gymnasium. "Yeah, that sounds like a lot of fun. Count me in."

After school, I headed to the football field for cheer practice. While we stretched, Dani drilled me on the words to some of the cheers I'd learned at our last practice.

"The 'Hit 'Em' cheer," she instructed.

I reached for my toes and recited the lines back to her. "Hit 'em, Hit 'em, knock them down. We're the Eagles, and we'll take your town."

"Good." Dani shifted to stretch her other leg. "Victory?"

"V-I-C-T-O-R-Y, victory, victory, that's our cry. Go, Eagles!"

"Bang Bang Choo Choo Train?"

I spread my legs wide on the grass and leaned forward to stretch the inside of my thighs. "Bang bang choo choo train, watch the Eagles do their thang—"

"Okay, girls," Coach called, interrupting me. "We're going to start by practicing the school song today."

"Hey, Dani," I said, pushing up from the ground as we headed to line up in our formation. "Would you be interested in helping me out with some of the other cheers outside of practice? I'm still missing something from that touchdown cheer."

"Sure thing. I'm not busy after practice if you want to stick around."

"Or we could go over to my house," I suggested.

"Five, six, seven, eight," Coach called, ending mine and Dani's conversation.

By the end of practice, I was again mentally exhausted, trying to remember all the moves and chants they'd taught me in the past week. Another week at it, and I might finally feel comfortable with the cheers. At least I was doing well with the stunts as a spotter.

"Ready?" Dani asked, slinging her bag over her shoulder and grabbing her pompons.

"As I'll ever be. Let me just tell Aaron I won't need a ride."

She again quizzed me on cheers on our way back to my house. I pushed my bike along slowly beside her. It wasn't the words that I was having trouble with; it was remembering which motions went to which cheers and which arm or leg went up at the right time.

"Don't worry so much," Dani told me when we reached my house. "We'll only stick with the easy cheers for Friday night since you, Rachel, and Tess are all new. That's, like, a third of the squad right there."

I wheeled my bike into the garage. "That's comforting, but I still feel so behind."

"You're doing great, though."

We entered the house through the garage, and I was surprised to see Parrot at my feet right away.

"Oh my gosh!" Dani's pitch rose. "Your cat is so pretty." She knelt to pet him.

I almost laughed, but it came out sounding like a grunt. "And hungry. He's only ever downstairs if he wants food. Otherwise, he sleeps on my bed."

Dani picked him up, but he struggled for his freedom. As soon as he heard the clink of the food against the side of his bowl as I poured it, he fought harder, and Dani dropped him. She laughed while he dug into his food.

I moved to the back doors that led to the patio and found my parents sitting outside. Mom held a book in her lap, and Dad typed on his laptop like usual.

I poked my head out the door. "Hey, I brought a friend over. I hope that's okay."

My parents turned and noticed Dani behind me.

"That's fine," my mom said, "but have her come out and meet us first."

I slid the door open further, and Dani nervously stepped closer. "Hi, uh, Maddie's parents." Her voice came out sounding more confident than her words.

They questioned her on cheerleading, who her parents were—they knew them, no surprise—and all of that. After a couple of minutes, I rescued her from my family's inquisition and told my parents we had to practice.

"There's some space in the living room if we move the coffee table," I offered.

Dani shrugged. "The living room is fine."

We ran through the cheers I was having trouble remembering, and then we practiced the school song before repeating it all again. After about forty-five minutes, I really felt like I was finally getting somewhere.

I dropped my pompons to the couch after our final run through with the school song and plopped my body down beside them. "Thank you for the one-on-one instruction, Dani. It really helped."

She fell to the cushion on the other end of the couch. "No problem. I should probably be getting home soon, though. I'm pretty hungry."

At the mention of food, I suddenly realized how hungry I was myself. "Hey, I'm not a savage! I have food in my cupboards, too. Let's go find something."

My parents had no doubt eaten before I arrived home, so it was another night of checking for leftovers or making my own dinner. I remembered how it used to be when my sisters were in high school. They were always out late for one thing or another, and my parents said that if they had to wait for everyone to be around at the same time, none of us would ever eat. Apparently they continued that tradition with me, but I honestly didn't mind.

I led Dani to the kitchen and opened the pantry in search of a meal idea. "Hungry for anything specific?"

"Really, Maddie, I can just eat at home."

The thing was, I was starting to like Dani, and I didn't have anything else to do tonight besides a math worksheet. It'd become awfully quiet around the house now that my sisters were off at college again.

"Dani, seriously. You're not intruding."

She seemed to accept this and eyed the food in my pantry. "Ooh, chocolate chips." She reached for the package.

I laughed. "If that's what you want…"

"No." She shook her head so that her brown pony tail

swayed from side to side. She set the bag back in the pantry. "I was just teasing."

"Actually," I reached for the bag, "we might be able to do something with this." I pulled a mixing bowl out from under the counter and began gathering ingredients.

"What are we making?" she asked curiously. "Cookies?"

I turned to her with a smile on my face. "Pancakes. It was something my sisters and I used to make all the time when we would stay up late on Friday nights."

Dani shifted to lean against the counter. "It sounds like you miss them."

"Make no mistake," I said, pointing my mixing spoon at her. "They're pains in my butt."

She threw her head back and laughed at me. "I know exactly what you mean, except my sisters are younger than me. Our tradition is strawberry-banana smoothie nights."

I raised my eyebrows. "Well, aren't we the healthy one?"

"Hey," she defended lightheartedly. "I can cheat every now and then." She turned to the ingredients on the counter. "So, what comes first in the recipe?"

Dani hung out at my house after practice the next two nights to help me with my cheers, and I finally began feeling comfortable with them. Alaina stopped by my house on Thursday night, the one night Dani didn't come over, and we caught up on everything I'd missed the past few days that she hadn't had a chance to discuss with me in art class. It wasn't anything special, but I began to miss my friends.

"I'll sit with you at lunch tomorrow. I promise," I told her before she left.

That night, I texted Logan again.

You can't avoid me forever. Can we talk?

I didn't hear back from him all night, but by the time I woke up, I found a text waiting from him.

There's nothing to talk about.

I sighed angrily as I rolled out of bed. This boy made no sense to me. If he was "fine" and "nothing was wrong," then why did it seem like he didn't want to be friends with me anymore? Lunch was going to be awkward.

By the time lunch arrived, I'd convinced Aaron to share me with my friends, and we found our way to my table. I purposely sat us on the opposite end of where Logan normally sat. Alaina jumped on the topic of our first major art assignment, and I spent my meal discussing ideas with her for our first sketch. I glanced at Logan a couple of times, but his eyes remained locked on his food in silence.

Will we ever be friends again? I wondered.

After school, I texted my parents telling them I was going to Aaron's house before the game and that, yes, his mom was going to be home.

I plopped down onto his couch. "So, is there anything fun to do around here?"

Aaron sat next to me and slung a muscular arm around my shoulder, pulling me into his warm chest. I could smell the Irish Spring soap he used. The scent made me go weak at the knees. Thank goodness I was already sitting down.

He touched his lips to the top of my head and wrapped his other arm around me in an embrace. "I'm fine just holding you," he said into my hair.

I curled into him and closed my eyes, simply enjoying every second of his company. We didn't move for a long time until his mother interrupted us several hours later asking if we were hungry. We ate, and then Aaron drove me to my house to change into my uniform and pick up my poms before heading to the game.

"You nervous?" he asked on the car ride to the field.

I immediately tensed my legs so they'd stop shaking. "That obvious?"

"Oh, come on. You'll do fine."

"I've never really performed in front of anyone before. My talent is drawing, not… being in front of people."

"Just keep your eyes on me. Cheer for me, and it'll be like no one else is there."

The thing is, he was probably right about that. It felt that way every time I looked at him.

"But I'll be facing the crowd for some of the cheers," I pointed out.

He squeezed my hand for encouragement. "You'll do great. Trust me."

And I almost did.

Once we reached the field, Aaron pulled me into a hug and planted a long kiss on my lips. All too soon, he had to escape to his team, and I had to find my squad.

Yell loud. Arms straight. What was the other one? Right. Clap on the beat.

And I did it all. I didn't miss a single step in the school song, and once we started cheers, the nervous patter of my heart had dropped back to its normal rate. It's not like the crowd was really watching us anyway. Their eyes looked straight through us onto the field, invested in the game. Even

Logan, who was sitting by the pep bad, seemed to be watching the game.

My heart flipped in my chest when Aaron prepared himself to kick a field goal. *That's my boyfriend*, I thought proudly.

"Go Aaron!" I yelled.

He caught my eye, and though it was hard to tell at this distance, I was sure he was smiling. He ran at the ball and sent it flying through the air. I held my breath as it soured in an arc. The split second it hung in the air felt like minutes. Finally, I released my breath when he made it. I jumped up and down in excitement.

After the Eagles won, Aaron found me on the field and pulled me into a hug.

"Congratulations!" I told him before brushing my lips against his.

"You were great," he said, finally releasing me.

I couldn't hide the blush rising to my cheeks. "Not as good as you are at football."

He playfully poked me in the ribs, and I recoiled with a laugh. "That's because you've only been practicing for a week. For some of us, it takes years to get good at something."

He poked me again, and I let out a yelp, playfully running from him. He chased after me and caught me at his vehicle, whipping me around and pressing me between his body and the cool metal of the car door. He paused for a moment, gazing down at my lips. The air between us seemed charged with energy, and suddenly, my body grew warm. I no longer noticed the chilly night breeze brushing across my exposed arms and legs. My breathing slowed, and then he pulled me into a passionate kiss.

CHAPTER 9

LOGAN

Classes seemed to come and go in a breeze, and I spent my days looking forward to lunch with Logan, art class, and—can you believe it?—choir. Emily nearly fell out of her chair in excitement when I told her I'd been placed in the soprano section. I struggled with sight reading at first, but once I heard the tune a couple of times, it wasn't hard to follow along.

Logan stopped me after the final bell rang Tuesday after choir. "Maddie?"

"Yeah?" I straightened the bottom of my shirt as I stood and looked at him. The blue eyes behind his glasses made me smile involuntarily.

"I was wondering if you'd be interested in learning more about music." He readjusted his glasses like he was nervous.

I stared at him in confusion for a moment. Was he offering because I was that bad and thought I needed the extra help?

"I just thought it'd give us a chance to spend more time together," he said when I didn't respond.

I quickly relaxed. More time with him sounded perfect. "Yeah, sure. What did you have in mind?"

He shrugged, but neither of us moved. "I thought maybe we could go in one of the practice rooms, and I could teach you a couple of things."

"Right now?"

"You aren't busy, are you?" he asked with a teasing smile.

"No, I'm not." I smiled back.

He began walking toward the nearest practice room. "Bring your folder along, and we'll take a look at some of the practice music."

I followed him and closed the door behind us. We settled beside each other on the bench in front of the piano. The room was cramped, to say the least, but it gave me an excuse to settle close to him. His knee warmed my own.

He flipped one of my music booklets open and situated it in front of us. "Okay, so the first thing you need to know is that every note on the line or between the lines has a name, a letter. They go A through G and then repeat. The easiest way to remember the notes between the lines is by the word FACE." He spelled out the word and pointed to where each note belonged. "Then the lines are EGBDF. Remember it as 'Every Good Boy Does Fine.'" He played a few notes on the piano to show me which sounds went with each note.

I raised my brows. "It's that easy?"

He laughed. "Not quite. There are also sharps and flats, and then each note is written out to tell you how long to hold it for. There's also different keys and time signatures."

"Aw man, this sounds hard. What's that for again?" I pointed to the symbol I recognized as a treble clef. Logan had explained it when he gave me my bracelet, but I couldn't remember what it meant.

"That's a treble clef. I wouldn't worry about that right now. It tells you what notes correspond to which line. So the notes I just explained only apply when you see that symbol—"

The door to our practice room popped opened, startling us both.

"Sorry," Alaina said, poking her head in. "I was looking for you guys. Jordan and I are going downtown for ice cream, and we were wondering if you wanted to tag along."

Logan and I exchanged a glance. As if we could communicate telepathically, we both knew exactly what each other was thinking.

I turned back to Alaina. "That sounds like fun. Count us in."

Minutes later, we were on our way downtown. Logan and Jordan walked a couple of paces ahead of Alaina and me. They discussed a musical I'd never heard of that was coming to the performing arts center.

"So." Alaina dragged out the word and wiggled her eyebrows at me. "What were you and Logan doing in the practice room?"

I ducked my head to hide my embarrassment. "Nothing. He was just teaching me about music."

"Right," she teased like she didn't believe me.

I pushed at her playfully.

"Didn't you learn how to play the recorder in fourth grade?" she asked.

"I forgot, okay?"

She pushed me back in the same manner, causing me to stumble and laugh.

"Cat fight!" Jordan joked.

I quickened my pace to walk beside Logan. Alaina only laughed harder when I shot her the evil eye in jest.

When we arrived at the ice cream shop, I ordered a chocolate chip cookie dough in a waffle cone, my favorite. I waited a few moments for Logan to place his order. Apparently I was standing too close, because when he turned with his cone in hand, he rammed right into me. His ice cream grazed the end of my nose.

"Hey," I exaggerated, scooping some of my own ice cream from my cone with my finger and wiping it across his nose. I couldn't help but laugh.

"That's not fair," he said with a smile. "Mine was an accident." He lifted a small amount of ice cream off his own cone, and I swiftly ducked out of the way.

"You'll have to catch me first." I darted out of the ice cream shop into the warm September sun and found a seat at one of the outdoor picnic tables. Logan exited the building behind me. I giggled uncontrollably as he tried to lick the ice cream off his nose. His tongue couldn't reach.

"Here," I offered, handing him the napkin that had been wrapped around my cone.

"Don't worry about it," he said, holding up his own.

"No more food fights," I warned, but I still hadn't stopped laughing.

My laughter instantly died when he looked at me. A warm sensation filled my chest, urging me to lean into him, to press my lips to his. He stared at me with a bright look in his eyes that told me he wanted the same thing. A second later, Alaina and Jordan plopped down at our table, pulling us both out of our trance.

"I was afraid one of you would drop your cone and we'd have to buy you another one," Jordan laughed.

"No," Alaina countered. "Their cones will probably melt while they're making puppy dog eyes at each other."

"We were not!" I defended, but even I knew that wasn't true.

Alaina turned to me while I quickly tried to catch the ice cream that was already melting on my cone. "I was thinking about doing some of the homecoming dress up days this year. Do you want to go as twins on twin day?"

"That sounds like fun. Any ideas on what kind of dress you want yet?"

The rest of the week passed by normally. I'd meet Logan at our lockers, and we'd head to homeroom together. My following classes would pass quickly, and then I'd hang out with my friends at lunch, never letting go of Logan's hand under the table. After school, Logan would try to teach me more about music until our choir instructor kicked us out so he could close up the music room. Afterwards, we'd hang out at the café or visit the music shop, milking every second of our time together as we could.

By the next week, I still couldn't get enough of him. I tagged along with him Tuesday afternoon to pick up his guitar, which he finally had enough money to buy. He pulled Lucy from the wall and strummed her a couple of times. She sounded like she was built using magic.

"So, what are you going to do with her now?" I asked once we returned to his car.

"Play her, of course. What else would I do?"

"Well, you could make videos and post them online or something. I'm sure you would get a good following."

Logan wiggled his brows at me. "Wouldn't you be jealous of all the fan girls?"

I wrinkled my nose, pretending I had to think about it. "Nah. I'd feel lucky because I'm the one who ended up with you."

He glanced at me, and his expression suddenly turned serious. "I'm the lucky one."

My heart flipped.

He dropped me off at home soon afterward, and I fell asleep dreaming of the last kiss we shared at my front door.

On Wednesday morning, I pedaled my bike to school. My first few classes passed normally, but I was caught off guard on my way to lunch.

"Maddie," Aaron called down the hall.

I turned to face him as he approached. The surface of my skin grew hot in anger. "If you're going to tell me one more time about how stupid I was to choose Logan—"

"I was going to," he interrupted, "but now I'm afraid you might kill me if you finish that sentence. How about I start by apologizing?"

My body immediately relaxed. Maybe there was hope that we could still be friends. "That would be a good place to start." I crossed my arms over my chest to show him I was serious.

Students rushed to the cafeteria, quickly leaving us in privacy.

"Look, we've known each other since we were kids. We've been really good friends for months." He averted his gaze from mine for several seconds before he finally looked up behind his dark lashes. "If I can't have you the way I want, I still hope we can be friends."

That's what I'd been trying to tell him all along! Only, I

didn't like the way he said, *If I can't have you the way I want.* It implied he still had feelings for me. We couldn't go back to being friends if he felt that way. Then again, if we were friends, he'd see that we could still enjoy each other's company without the romance.

"So, friends?" he asked.

"Friends," I agreed.

Even though Aaron had apologized and we'd agreed to be friends, we didn't have much of a chance to actually talk to each other. Since we only had one class together and sat on opposite sides of the room, we didn't chat like we used to. We texted a little bit here and there, but it seemed like forced conversation. I had to wonder if we'd ever get our true friendship back. At least his texts about how I chose the wrong guy had stopped.

For the most part, however, I didn't really think about it. I noticed him in the halls and at lunch, and I thought about him every time I received a text from him, but otherwise, my thoughts were dedicated to Logan.

I only realized how much I'd been consumed by Logan's company on Friday in art class. Alaina flipped open her sketchbook beside me. My first thought was that her flower drawing was beautiful, but a moment later, a string of curse words went off like firecrackers in my mind.

"Crap. That's due today." I quickly flipped open my sketchbook and tried to remember if I'd drawn anything in the past week. The last drawing in my book had already been graded. "Think I can draw something in the next ten minutes before he calls my name to check my book?"

Alaina stared back at me, her brows raised and her mouth slightly open.

"What?" I asked innocently.

She finally found her voice. "How did *you* not finish this assignment?"

"I guess I forgot." I quickly pulled my pencil out and began drawing the first thing that came to mind: Logan's eyes. By the time our teacher called my name, I at least had an outline drawn.

Mr. Brown frowned at me. "This isn't finished, Miss Rose."

I brushed a strand of brown hair from my eyes. "I'm really sorry. I…" I had no excuse.

"You know, when you get into college, your professors won't give you second chances."

I'd heard my teachers give this lecture to other students before. How could I be so stupid to miss such an easy assignment? "I know. I'm sorry."

He flipped my notebook shut and handed it back to me, still frowning. "Be sure it doesn't happen again."

I shamefully returned to my seat, angry at myself.

CHAPTER 10

AARON

Between classes and cheer practice, it never felt like I had enough time with Aaron. We hung out on the way to school, at lunch, and after practice, but the car rides were far too short since I only lived a couple of blocks from the school.

On Thursday morning, I spotted Logan down a few lockers from mine. As if he could feel my eyes on him, he looked up and met my gaze. He didn't look away immediately like normal but actually gave me a half smile. It made me believe, if only briefly, that maybe he'd forgiven me and we could slowly return to being friends.

Later that day, Aaron and I sat at my table for lunch. I found a seat next to Alaina. Logan sat on her opposite side.

"What did you guys get on your physics quiz?" Emily asked. "Is it just me, or does the new science teacher seem like a really tough grader?"

"How can he be tough?" Logan asked. "You just put in an answer, and it's either right or wrong."

Emily shrugged from across the table. "There were some essay questions, and I didn't do well on those."

"I agree," I told her. "I didn't do well on those questions, either."

I glanced at Logan, but he stared down at his fruit like he didn't hear me. I continued trying to engage in the conversation, but every time I voiced my thoughts, Logan shut down and gazed at his tray instead of talking with the rest of us.

By the end of lunch, my jaw was beginning to hurt from clenching it in anger at Logan. My frustrations only grew as the school day wore on. I continued to replay his reaction in my mind. How could he still be so mad at me that he wouldn't even talk around me? And why did he have to trick me with that half smile earlier like things were getting better between us?

I cornered him at his locker after school. "You need to stop this," I told him sternly.

"Stop what?" His tone remained even like he honestly didn't know what I was talking about.

I crossed my arms and spoke quickly. "You need to stop shutting me out. You don't want to be friends anymore. I get that. But can we stop acting like we're enemies? Yes, I'm going to sit at your lunch table every now and then because, like it or not, I'm still friends with everyone there. We're going to have to learn to live with each other because I'm not going to stop being friends with everyone else just because you decided you didn't want to talk to me anymore. We don't have to be friends with each other, but stop acting like you can't be part of the group when I'm around." I sucked in a deep breath.

Logan sheepishly gazed down at his feet. His voice came out as almost a whisper. "I'm sorry."

My heart nearly broke as I suddenly realized how hard this

must be for him. I relaxed the tense muscles in my shoulders. "Look, I'm sorry, too. I just wish things didn't have to be this way. Can't we go back to being friends?"

He finally looked at me. "I'll try." His features seemed to light up like he actually accepted that being friends was the best option for us.

"I really hope you mean it," was the last thing I said to him before I headed off down the hall on my way to cheerleading practice.

"These car rides are too short," I complained to Aaron when we pulled up to my house after practice.

Dani sat in the back. She'd come over to help me with some new cheers we were performing at tomorrow's away game.

Aaron leaned over so I could feel his breath on the side of my face. "I know." His lips grazed against my cheek.

"Yuck! Get a room!" Dani teased.

Aaron turned to her. "Like I haven't seen you and Brandon make out enough times."

I witnessed Dani's cheeks grow red in the mirror, and she quickly pressed her lips together. She opened her door. "I'll be inside."

Aaron focused his attention back on me. "Too bad we can't sit together on the way to the game tomorrow."

It was cool that we got to cheer at away games since most of the cheerleading squads in our conference only cheered at home games. Not even all the schools had cheerleaders because they were all so small. But sadly, our cheerleaders had to ride a separate bus than the football players. It didn't feel like I was spending as much time with Aaron as I initially thought cheerleading would allow.

My face fell, and Aaron noticed.

He tucked a strand of hair behind my ear. "Hey, don't worry about it. We can spend Saturday together."

Immediately, my heart leapt. "I'd love that!"

"Okay," he agreed. "I'll see you tomorrow, my angel."

He left a kiss on my lips before I exited the car. I stood there in my driveway as I watched him leave, my pompons held tightly against my chest.

"Maddie!" Dani called from the front door, pulling me from my dreamy state.

I whirled toward her. "Coming!"

She laughed at me. "Girl, you've got it bad." She stretched out the word "bad."

I didn't say anything while I pushed the coffee table out of the middle of the living room. Hopefully she couldn't see the blush in my cheeks. When I was satisfied that embarrassment was no longer written all over my face, I turned back to her. "Ready?"

Dani helped me run through a couple of new cheers I'd learned that week, and within the next half hour, my confidence grew.

"I think I'm getting it," I told her.

"Well, you're a fast learner, and you're willing to go above and beyond. None of the other new girls even ask for extra help." Dani plopped down onto my couch. "It's kind of disappointing because it seems like no one else cares."

I sat beside her. "You seem to care a lot."

"And that's why I'm captain," she teased. "Hey, do you want to learn this cool cheer we're teaching you guys next week?

We want to do it for the homecoming game, but it's kind of hard."

I hopped up from the couch. "Sure! I'll take a head start on it."

Dani situated herself in the center of the floor and began stomping her feet and clapping. "Just join in. I'll teach you the words after you get the beat down."

I stared at her feet hopelessly.

"Come on," she encouraged, never missing a beat. "It's easiest to learn by just doing it."

"Okay," I agreed uncertainly. I stood beside her and watched her feet move, listening intently to the beat. When I noticed the rhythm repeating, I attempted to join in. I probably looked like I was having a stroke.

Dani burst out laughing. "Okay, okay. We'll take it slow."

She tried again but couldn't help but giggle at me. In the next moment, we were both laughing hysterically, so much that Dani couldn't keep herself steady and fell to couch clutching her stomach.

The doorbell rang just then, and I headed to answer it, still laughing. When I opened the door, I found Alaina standing on the other side.

She pulled her eyebrows together. "What's so funny?"

I drew the door open wider to let her in. "Dani and I are practicing cheers, and, well, I kind of suck." I glanced back at Dani, who was still laughing at me.

Alaina stepped into the house. Her eyes shifted between me in the doorway and Dani on the couch. "Uh, okay. I just came over to hang out… if that's okay." Her voice came out uneven.

"Of course it is. We were almost done anyway."

Dani's laughter died down, and she stood to gather her

things. "Yeah, no. It's perfectly fine. I was just about to get going."

"You don't want dinner?" I asked.

"No, it's fine," she answered, slinging her bag over her shoulder. "I think I've eaten enough of your food in the past two weeks. I'll see you tomorrow for the game."

"Okay. Bye," I told her as she headed out the door.

She turned back one last time at the bottom of the steps and shouted with a raised pom, "Go Eagles!"

"Go Eagles!" I shouted back. I shut the door and turned to Alaina. Her expression had fallen, and my tone quickly shifted to one of concern. "What's wrong?"

She looked up from the nail she was biting and shrugged. "I don't know. It's just weird seeing you in cheerleader mode. You seem... different."

"What?" I asked, my voice a little higher than normal. "I haven't changed at all."

I expected her to retort back, but instead, she just dropped her eyes. "Never mind. Forget I said anything."

I held my jaw open in disbelief. Was she *mad* at me? She was almost acting like it. But I didn't know what else to say on the subject, so I just asked her, "So, are you hungry?"

"I guess I could use something." She followed behind me to the kitchen. "Hey, you didn't still want to put anything into the show for the art night, did you? Because it's next Friday, and I'm pretty sure you need to get your art in by tomorrow."

I sucked in a quick breath. "Crap."

Alaina leaned against my kitchen counter. "What?"

"You just reminded me about our sketches due tomorrow for art class! I totally forgot to draw something." I rushed back into the living room and pulled my sketchbook out of my bag, flipping to the next available page. I spoke as I headed back into the kitchen. "I need to draw something before tomorrow."

"Uh, okay. Are you going to have supper?"

I shrugged. "I guess we could make something quick like grilled cheese."

Alaina headed around the counter but paused briefly. She turned back to me like she had something to say, but she didn't speak. She simply tapped what was left of her gnawed off fingernails on the counter top.

I gave her a questioning look.

She sighed. "It's just... you seem so preoccupied lately. Normally you'd have ten drawings done in a week, and this week, you don't even have one." She gestured to my open sketchbook on the counter.

I stared down at the blank page. "I guess cheerleading is taking up some time. Aaron and I hung out a couple of times, too."

She shifted her weight between her feet. "Okay, well, I just don't want to see you give up your art for anything."

"Give up my art? Don't worry. I'd never do that." Except the problem was that I was already drifting away from my artwork.

CHAPTER 11

LOGAN

The Friday of Alaina's art night arrived the third week of school. I originally planned to bike over there, but at the last minute, I texted Alaina for a ride and tagged along with her.

"Why's it at the library?" I wondered aloud on our way there.

Alaina shrugged. The dangly earrings she wore to match her blue dress—and headband, of course—moved with her motions. I hadn't dressed up, but I figured I looked okay when I glanced at my jeans and cute pink top.

"It's probably because they didn't have anywhere else to do it," Alaina answered. "The library is, like, the only thing the town owns besides the town hall and the park. The guy said something about bringing the arts together—like literature and visual art or something."

"I'm sure it'll be cool."

Alaina nodded. "Yeah."

She pulled into the parking lot of the library, and we walked inside together. I couldn't remember the last time I'd been there—probably when I was in elementary school—but it seemed different with all the artwork on the walls. The smell hadn't changed, though. I inhaled the scent of old books, a complementary aroma of paper, ink, and glue. The lilies on the front counter interrupted my moment of nostalgia. There weren't many people there when we entered, but Alaina bounced on her toes in excitement nonetheless.

"Look," she pointed, "that lady is looking at my painting!"

I glanced across the room and noticed Alaina's painting immediately. Even if I hadn't seen it before, I would be able to tell it was hers by the brushstrokes. This particular painting was one of her favorites. It was of Jordan's cocker spaniel, Lady.

"Think she'll buy it?" I asked.

"Well, they're supposed to be hanging for a couple of weeks. We'll see what happens after they announce the top three pieces next week."

I slowly walked along the outside wall to inspect the artwork. When I saw what was there, I realized that I could have easily entered a drawing and have done well. Even little kids had entered their art. Disappointment washed over me, and I cursed myself for not taking the chance. Even Logan had more artistic talent with the bracelet he made me than some of the drawings here. I glanced down at the purple string around my wrist. I guess there's only so much talent in a small town.

After viewing the first couple of pieces, I spoke to Alaina confidently. "I'm sure you'll win."

She paced a few steps ahead of me. "Check this out."

She pointed to a painting of the sunset on the wall. I recognized the barn in the painting. It stood just outside of town.

"Wow. That's one of the best I've seen so far, besides yours, of course."

She shrugged. "I didn't enter my painting thinking I was going to be the best. I just wanted to share my art with people. Besides, it's good marketing."

She turned away so I couldn't see her face, but I knew her well enough to sense the lie and disappointment in her voice. She clearly thought the painting of the barn was better than hers of Lady. I didn't agree, though. Something about the colors in the sunset weren't right.

I followed Alaina down the aisle and past paintings, drawings, photographs, printmaking, macramé, and tons of other works of visual art. There were even a couple of ceramics lined along the tops of the shelves where the library's featured books usually sat. Her enthusiasm grew the more we walked.

Slowly, more people trickled into the building to see what type of artistic talent our town residents brought to the community. The room began to buzz with chatter.

"This is awesome," I told Alaina. "Lots of people will see your painting and love it."

"That's why we have to vote." She took my hand excitedly.

At the front of the library, they had a poll going, asking you to vote on your three favorite pieces of art. Alaina handed me a card and a pencil to write down my favorites.

"You don't have to vote for mine," she told me humbly, but she knew I'd vote for her anyway. It wasn't just that I was her best friend; I actually really liked her painting.

I wrote down two other votes, one for a painted ceramic, and one for a photograph of a flower garden. I slid my piece of paper into the box where they were collecting votes, and then I turned to Alaina. "So, what do you get if you win?"

She deposited her vote and then adjusted the headband in

her hair. "Bragging rights, I guess." Her eyes scanned the room. "I think I should go talk to some people. Oh, look! There's the guy who told me about it. I should thank him."

Alaina hurried off, leaving me unsure of what to do next. I slumped into a chair in one of the reading areas to wait for her. I glanced around, and that guilt for not entering one of my own drawings fell over me again. This night would have been a lot more fun if I had participated, but instead, I sat distanced from it all in my own little corner.

To kill time, I pulled out my phone and texted Logan.

How's the game?

I was never really one for following sports, but if it wasn't for Alaina's art night, I'd be there with Logan just so I could spend more time with him. Last Friday was an away game, and Logan didn't have to play at those, so we'd spent some time together. Tonight, though, he was stuck playing in the band and couldn't make it here with me.

Haven't even started yet, he texted back.

Having any fun?

As soon as we start playing, I will be. You should come.

My heart fell. Sure, I wanted to support Alaina, but now that I'd already made it to her art night, I wondered if I could skip out on the rest of it and spend time with Logan. Except Alaina was my ride. I glanced toward her and noticed Jordan had arrived. He stood by her side, and they both laughed at something the old guy across from them was saying. He must have been the guy who encouraged Alaina to enter her painting. Now that Jordan was here, there was no chance Alaina would be leaving any time soon.

Sorry, I texted. *You know I'm hanging out with Alaina tonight.*

Yeah. Maybe we can hang out tomorrow.

My pulse quickened. A whole day with Logan outside of school? Sign me up!

I'd love to. What do you have in mind?

Surprise?

I didn't particularly like surprises, but a surprise from Logan was better than nothing at all.

Sounds like fun, I answered.

See you in the morning, babe.

Can't wait.

Alaina seemed drained by the time the night was over, so much that her eyes began drooping on the way back home.

"You okay?" I asked.

She blinked a couple of times. "Yeah, I'm fine. Just tired." She pulled into my driveway.

I hopped out of the car. "Thanks for the ride!" I waved back at her and hurried into the house.

After dropping my purse onto my desk and falling onto my pillow, I realized how tired *I* was. I breathed a heavy sigh and dragged myself to my dresser, where I pulled out my pajamas. Once I lay back down, I fell asleep almost instantly.

Logan rang my doorbell the next morning just as I pulled on my jeans after getting out of the shower.

"Can you get that?" I yelled down to my dad, who I knew was sitting in his home office next to the front door. "It should be Logan."

"Are you sure you want me to get it?" he called back up the stairs. "I might embarrass you."

Heat rose to my face. He was only teasing, but he was also right. I quickly threw a t-shirt over my head and raced down the stairs past my dad, who already had a finger on the door handle.

"Never mind, Dad. I've got this."

He strolled back into his office with a laugh.

I pulled the door open. Logan's smiling face made my knees go weak. I didn't even care that my hair was still wet and I didn't have any makeup on. I pulled him into a hug as soon as I saw him.

"I missed you," I whispered into his ear, even though we saw each other at school yesterday. Somehow, that seemed like ages ago.

He squeezed me back. "I missed you, too. You don't seem ready to go."

I pulled away, but the smile on my face didn't waver. "I'm almost ready. Let me go brush my hair."

Logan stepped into my house, and I raced upstairs and threw my hair into a ponytail in record time. I quickly slipped on my flip flops and grabbed my purse from where it sat on my desk.

I adjusted the strap on my shoulder at the bottom of the stairs. "Ready?"

Logan nodded before taking my hand.

"Dad, I'm leaving," I called into the next room. "See you sometime tonight."

"Okay," he replied. "Don't be home too late. Have fun!"

On my way to Logan's car, I realized something. Normally my parents asked where we were going and what we'd be doing, but my dad didn't this time.

I slid into the passenger seat. "Does my dad know about the surprise?"

Logan's lips twitched into a smile. "I told him while you were upstairs."

My eyes widened. "He talked to you? He didn't say anything embarrassing, did he?"

Logan pulled out of the driveway. "Of course not, babe. What would he say anyway? You have nothing to be embarrassed about in front of me."

I buried my face in my hands at the thought of my father talking to my boyfriend. Once I dropped them, I spoke. "I don't know. He's my dad. He's bound to come up with something."

A laugh escaped Logan's lips. "You have nothing to worry about." He squeezed my hand for reassurance.

I squinted out the window to see if I could tell where he was taking me. "So, where are we going?"

Logan circled his thumb on the back of my hand. "I told you, it's a surprise."

"You and your surprises," I complained before shooting him a teasing smile.

We drove out of town, and after another fifteen minutes, Logan turned down a road I'd never been down. I studied the scenery, wondering where he could possibly be taking me. A thick forest lined the road, and the long stretch in front of us didn't seem to show any promise. We passed by a couple of houses, and I half expected him to pull into one of the driveways, but he continued driving along the narrow road. He turned a couple more times, but I didn't bother prodding him about where we were going. I knew he wouldn't tell me anyway.

When he turned down a dirt road, I finally spoke up. "Logan, are you lost?"

He glanced at me before looking back at the road in front of him. He bounced in his seat with every pot hole we drove over. "Of course I'm not lost. Don't worry; we're almost there."

The trees didn't seem to end, but the road did. It widened into a circle, either for turning around or parking; I wasn't sure. At first, I thought maybe Logan was lying and he really *was* lost. Maybe he was going to turn around and find a way back to the main road. Instead, he stopped the car at the end of the road and shifted it into park.

"This is it?" I scanned the trees.

Logan reached into the back seat and pulled his backpack onto his lap. "Yep."

"But there's nothing here."

He opened his door and stepped out of the car, slinging his backpack over his shoulder. "Sure there is. Come on."

I warily followed him out of the car. He held his hand out to me, so I grabbed onto it while he led me over to the trees. I looked around again, trying to spot an indication of what we were doing here. When my eyes fell back in front of me, I noticed a long stretch of dirt cutting its way through the trees. Sunlight streamed through the canopy, casting rays of light on the narrow trail. Logan released my hand to walk in front of me. He talked while we walked, mostly about music. It helped occupy my mind, so I didn't focus on how far we'd gone. When my feet started to ache in my flip flops, though, I began to notice the distance.

If he didn't have to keep it a surprise, I thought, *I would have worn better shoes.*

I didn't say anything out loud because in the next moment, a distant noise caught my attention. I stopped in my tracks. After a few paces, Logan noticed I was no longer following him.

"Do you hear that?" I asked. I couldn't quite pinpoint what

it was. It almost sounded like a strong wind rustling through the trees, but there was only a light breeze.

A grin broke across Logan's face. "Come on. We're almost there."

He quickened his pace, and even though I was starting to form a blister on the side of my right foot, I followed just a step behind him. Soon, the trees began to thin. The sound I'd heard a moment ago grew louder. A split second before I saw the water, I realized what it was. Logan and I emerged into a small clearing along the banks of a river. A couple of yards upstream stood a small waterfall. It was only a few feet high, but the way the river twisted through the surrounding greenery was breathtaking.

"Wow," was all I could say.

"Pretty, right?"

I couldn't tear my gaze from the landscape even as Logan took my hand to pull me further into the clearing.

"How did you find this place?" I finally asked.

He shrugged. "It's not exactly a secret. It's a public place, but I guess people don't appreciate it as much as they used to. My family used to hike out here once a year or so just to enjoy it."

I was so focused on the scenery that I hadn't noticed Logan start to unpack his backpack. When I finally looked over at him, he had a small blanket laid out in front of the river.

"Sit down," he encouraged.

I kicked off my flip flops next to his blanket and sank down onto it, crossing my legs. Logan sat across from me and dug into his backpack. He pulled out three plastic containers and set them between us before grabbing two plastic bags from his pack. He handed me one of the bags, and I stared down at the sandwich in it. My heart fluttered at the sweet gesture.

"All this was about a picnic?" I asked.

Logan nodded. "You don't like tomato, do you? Because I didn't put it on your sandwich."

I smiled back at him. "You're so sweet, and you're right. I don't like tomato." I unwrapped my sandwich and bit into it. A light breeze blew through my hair during the silence that followed. I inhaled the scent of nature around me. "It's really peaceful out here. Thanks for bringing me."

Logan shifted to lean on one hand while his other held his sandwich. He gazed out toward the water. "It really is. That's why I wanted to show it to you."

"What's in the containers?" I gestured toward them.

Logan smiled before swallowing a bite of his sandwich. "If you're still hungry, I have potato salad, some mixed fruit, and some of my mom's famous Rice Crispy bars."

"Mm, Rice Crispy."

Mostly, we sat in silence, listening to the flow of water next to us and enjoying the beautiful weather. After we finished eating and Logan packed his food away, I shifted closer to him, and he took me into his arms. We lay together on the blanket and stared up at the sky. His arms warmed my body—both inside and out—like it was where I was meant to be.

"That one looks like a butterfly." He pointed to an approaching cloud.

"Agreed, but check out that one. It kind of looks like a unicorn."

Logan tilted his head. "I guess I can see that. Now the butterfly just kind of looks like a blob."

I laughed. We lay there for what must have been hours,

just talking and imagining shapes out of the clouds. A chill overcame me when he finally pulled away and announced that it was time to pack up and head back to the car. I didn't want to; I wanted this beautiful day to last forever.

"Wait," I said before he could stand.

He stared back at me expectantly. I didn't really know what I had stopped him for, but I didn't have to think long about it. I leaned into him and wrapped my arms around his neck. I felt his body relax when our lips touched. What felt like far too soon, we drew away from each other and stood. My blister ached in reminder of the long walk back.

When we reached the car, I grabbed my purse from the floor near my feet and set it on my lap. "Does our date really have to be over?" I asked in disappointment.

Logan's soft eyes met mine. "Of course it doesn't, but we'll have plenty of time to spend together next weekend at the homecoming dance."

A surge of adrenaline shot through my veins at the reminder. "Crap!" I shouted louder than I intended. I quickly dug into my purse in search of my phone.

Logan started up the car and glanced over at me. "What's wrong?"

"I completely forgot! I was supposed to meet up with Alaina, Emily, and Holly to go dress shopping today." I pulled my wallet from my purse to give myself more room to search for my phone. *Why hadn't Alaina sent me a text reminding me?* I wondered.

Logan drove down the dirt road. "I'm sorry. I didn't realize. Do you want to see if they're still shopping?"

Finally, my hands clamped around the phone, and I pressed the home button to wake it up, but the screen remained blank. My face tensed so much that I began to form a headache. I couldn't believe I'd ditched my friends. "I was so tired last night that I forgot to charge my phone. It's dead. Can I use yours to text Alaina?"

Logan pulled his phone from his pocket and handed it to me.

I began typing a message before I noticed the small symbol at the top of his notifications bar. "Dang it. There's no service out here."

A couple of minutes later, a bar finally popped up, and Logan's phone chimed several times.

"Who texted me?" he asked, giving me permission to read the messages to him.

One was from Jordan that I didn't read, and the other three were from Alaina. She asked Logan if he was with me or knew where I was. I quickly texted her back explaining how my phone died and I forgot about dress shopping.

Are you still shopping? I texted.

We're already done. I called your house, and your parents said you were with Logan, so we went shopping without you.

I'm so sorry.

Alaina didn't text back, and I wasn't sure if that was a sign of forgiveness or because she was mad at me. My gut told me it was the latter. Guilt overcame me, and I asked Logan to drive me home.

I sulked into the house. In my bedroom, I plugged my phone in and waited for it to come alive so I could check the messages Alaina sent. She started by asking if I needed a ride, then told me she was waiting for me at the mall, and then asked several times where I was. I slumped to my bed, feeling a sickness in my stomach for the way I had ditched my friends. It was so unlike me to forget about them.

A few minutes later, the doorbell rang. I didn't think

anything of it until I heard Alaina's voice echoing up the stairs along with my father's. I exited my room and slunk down the stairs to greet her, praying she wasn't too mad at me. Her arms crossed over her chest, and she raised an eyebrow at me. Nobody said anything as she headed past my dad and followed me up to my bedroom.

I plopped down on my bed. "Alaina, I'm *really* sorry." I knew I deserved whatever lecture she was about to give me.

She stood in my doorway with a stone cold expression on her face. Her arms never dropped from their position over her chest. "I'm not mad that you spent the day with Logan," she finally said. "I'm mad that you didn't tell us about it and just ditched the rest of us."

I hung my head guiltily. "I didn't mean to. I forgot about it. We hung out last night, and you didn't mention anything about it. I just forgot."

"I was tired last night," she pointed out in defense. "Besides, it's not like you to flake like that."

A brief pause filled the silence, but I couldn't bring myself to say anything. I didn't have any real excuse.

Alaina pursed her lips when I didn't respond. She sighed deeply like the next thing she was about to say was too difficult for her. She managed to spit it out confidently. "You're changing yourself too much for Logan."

My gaze flew to hers. I was not! How could she say something like that? "I'm not changing. I'm still the same old Maddie."

Her brows shot up. "The same old Maddie? The one who stops drawing and forgets about her art homework? The one who's all of a sudden interested in music when she's never cared about it before? The one who ditches her friends without telling them where she is?"

I looked back at my hands because I couldn't bear to meet her gaze.

"You know," she continued, "I thought that Aaron would be the bad one for you. I guess I was wrong."

Then she whirled around and left my room. I heard the front door click shut behind her, but there was nothing I could do about it now except reflect on her words.

CHAPTER 12

AARON

The third week of school was filled with classes, cheerleading practice, and hanging out with Aaron afterward. After school on Friday, I stopped by Dani's locker. When she noticed my approach, she spun around so that her long dark ponytail flipped over to the opposite shoulder.

"Ready for tonight's game?" she asked enthusiastically.

I bit my lip. "Not really. I'm a little nervous about the new dynamite cheer."

Dani and I fell into step beside each other.

"Well, I have plans with Brandon, but I can stop by your house shortly before the game, and we can run through it a few times if you want."

"That'd be great! Thank you. And maybe we could work a little on our English project, too."

"No problem." In that moment, she spotted Brandon. She hurried ahead of me and turned back to wave. "See you in a couple of hours."

I headed down the hall toward Aaron's locker. Since

neither of us had to be anywhere before the game, I suggested we spend some time together.

"What do you want to do?" he asked on the walk to his car.

I shrugged. "Ice cream?"

Aaron gave a sideways smile. "Sounds great."

I ordered a cookies and cream cone, and Aaron got strawberry. We slid into a booth in the corner and licked at our ice cream while discussing our groups' English projects.

"No stealing our ideas," I warned him.

He laughed with confidence. "Please, like we'd need to steal from you. Our project is going great." After another lick of his cone, he asked, "How are your other classes going?"

"Okay, I guess. I didn't do great on my latest science test, and my government class sucks. But other than that, I guess I'm doing okay so far."

"How's art treating you this semester?" he asked before biting into his ice cream. The idea of using my teeth on ice cream made me shiver.

I pressed my lips together guiltily.

"What?" He dragged the word out as if he was suspicious of me, but he smiled to show he was only teasing. His dimple appeared, which was something I loved about him.

"I, um, almost forgot about one of my assignments last week," I admitted sheepishly. I hadn't thought to mention this to him earlier. It was the first time the subject came up.

"Maddie," he sighed like he was disappointed in me.

I rolled my eyes. "Okay, I'm making it out to be worse than it was. I remembered the night before it was due, and I whipped something up real quick." I shrugged and then spoke smugly. "I still got full points."

"Well, that makes it all right," he said before rolling his eyes back at me. "It's not because of me, is it?"

"What?" I asked, shocked. "No, of course not. Why would you think that?"

He bit into his cone and then wiped his face with his napkin before he spoke. "I admit we've been spending a lot of time together. I wouldn't want your grades to suffer. You still want to get into a good college, don't you?"

Why did he suddenly sound like my father?

"What? No, Aaron. My grades are fine. I've just been spending a lot of time doing other stuff, like cheerleading."

"You like it, right?" he asked.

It almost sounded like he was worried, like he wasn't sure it was the right choice to drag me into it. Except if I was being honest, I *did* enjoy cheerleading. Well, parts of it, at least. I was having a lot of fun with Dani.

"Yeah, Aaron. I like it." I hoped that was the end of the conversation. When I glanced back down at my ice cream, a soft, melted layer had formed over the top. I licked it off before it could drip onto my hand.

Luckily, the topic didn't come up again. Aaron dropped me off at home a couple hours later. He left me with a kiss, promising he'd see me shortly for the game. I set my purse on the couch and headed upstairs to change into my cheerleading uniform while waiting for Dani to arrive. Just as I zipped up my skirt, the doorbell rang. I hurried downstairs to answer it.

"Ready?" I asked when I opened the door.

"Okay," Dani answered in her best cheerleader voice.

I laughed as she stepped into the house. "You're the one who says 'ready.'"

She shrugged with a giggle. "I know, but I couldn't resist. Okay, let's run through that cheer."

The extra practice with Dani helped immensely, and by the time Aaron arrived back at my house to drive us to the game, a newfound confidence in the cheers had settled over me.

I slipped on my sneakers and grabbed my pompons and purse off the couch. "Anything else I need?"

Dani glanced around as if to make sure I hadn't dropped anything. "I don't think so. You have your poms and your uniform. You should be good."

Once we arrived at the field, Aaron kissed me goodbye, and Dani and I hurried to the sidelines to join our other squad mates. I tossed my purse near the edge of the fence in the pile of other cheerleaders' bags. A chill settled over the field as the sun fell low in the sky, but it wasn't quite cold enough for goosebumps.

"Anyone need to run through some cheers before the game?" Dani asked. Even though we both knew there were a couple of girls who could use the extra help, no one answered. "Do you all remember what stunts we're doing?"

"Can you remind me?" Rachel asked.

We reviewed what we were doing for the game until the pep band began playing. I noticed Logan in the stands, but my anger for his behavior had mostly faded. He caught my eye once or twice, but that tension in his features didn't seem as strong as it'd been last week. It was like he was starting to forgive me, or at least learning to live with it.

Blake sat next to Logan with a camera slung around his neck. He noticed me looking their way, so he smiled and waved. That got me to smile just before he pulled the camera up to snap a shot for the yearbook. I made a big deal of rolling my eyes at him so he could see from this distance. He only laughed back and snapped another picture of me. My heart sank when the moment ended. Since I'd been sitting by Aaron at lunch most days, I hadn't hardly talked to Blake since school started. I missed him.

Announcements rang over the speakers, and I turned with my team toward the flag to prepare for the national anthem. Once the game started, I focused my attention on the field. My gaze drifted toward Aaron every chance I got, even when he was only standing on the sidelines.

After the game, Dani came up to me. "You did really well tonight, Maddie."

I shot her back a smile. "Thank you. You've been a big help."

"It's no problem. See you next week!" She waved as she retreated to meet up with her boyfriend.

Aaron found me on the sidelines and pulled me into a hug. "Hey, angel."

I smiled back. "You guys did really good tonight." His face was so close that I could feel his breath on mine. It sent my body melting into his. I wrapped my arms around him tighter.

He pulled away far too soon. "Are you ready to go?"

"Do I have to?" I faked a pout.

"I can go home and change and then come back to your house. Your parents probably won't mind, will they?"

I took Aaron's hand and shook my head. "No. I'm sure they'll let you hang out for a while, as long as your parents don't care."

"Nah. My parents don't really give me a curfew."

"Lucky," I teased.

We reached his car, and Aaron drove me home. When we approached my house, I noticed Alaina's car in my driveway.

"Oh," Aaron said. "Did you already have plans?"

I was just as confused as he was. Alaina knew I'd be at the game, but maybe she just wanted to hang out after her...

"Crap!" I shouted out loud.

Aaron pulled into my driveway beside Alaina's car. "What's wrong?"

I bit my lip. Alaina's art night was tonight, and I was supposed to visit her for a little bit before the game. Instead, I had Dani come over and help me with that cheer. Plus, my phone had been in my purse during the whole game, so if she texted me, I didn't hear any of the notifications. I quickly dug my phone out of my purse and checked the screen. Sure enough, she'd left several texts already.

I took a deep breath and turned back to Aaron. "Nothing. It's fine."

His hands dropped from the steering wheel. "You still want me to come back?"

My eyes shifted between Aaron and the front door. I let out a sigh. "Yeah, you can come back. I just need to talk to Alaina for a couple of minutes."

"Okay. Hey," he stopped me before I could get out of the car, "is something wrong between you two?"

I twisted my face up uncertainly. "I think everything will be fine. Don't worry about it."

"Okay," he agreed before pulling me back toward him and planting a kiss on my lips.

"I'll see you soon," I called back to him.

When I turned toward the front door, guilt knotted in my chest. Alaina was going to be *so* mad at me. How could I have ditched her on her special night? I had the urge to flee, to not face the guilt, but when I glanced back at Aaron, he was already pulling out of the driveway. I had to face Alaina, but there was nothing I could say to make up for forgetting about her big night.

I stepped through the door cautiously. Just as I suspected,

Alaina was sitting in my living room waiting for me. A stone cold expression sat on her face. I thought I'd be able to manage an apology, but once I saw her, I couldn't bring myself to speak. She stared at me like she expected me to talk first. I let my face fall, hoping she'd see that I realized my wrongdoings. I hated knowing that I'd disappointed her.

Finally, she stood and broke the silence with a snappy tone to her voice. "How could you bail on me?"

I winced like she'd slapped me. I deserved that. I cleared my throat. "I'm sorry."

"An hour," she stated. "An hour is all I asked from you. I wanted to spend just an hour with my best friend before you had to go to the game. You were supposed to meet me there. I waited and waited, and you never showed."

"I forgot." I knew it wasn't a valid excuse.

Alaina's voice rose, and I only hoped my parents weren't listening to our conversation. "What's gotten into you lately?"

I took a step back, startled. "What do you mean?"

She narrowed her eyes. "Before this school year, I could have counted on you for anything. Now you're ditching me? You didn't even bother to text me that you couldn't make it?"

"I didn't hear my phone while I was cheering." I said it like I had a good reason, like she should forgive me, but the anger written on her face told me it was going to take much more than excuses to make up for this. "I'm sorry, Alaina. It was one mistake."

"It's not just that," she spat back before I could hardly finish my sentence. "You're completely different, Maddie. You don't sit by us at lunch. It's like—"

"I do sit by you!" I defended.

She scoffed. "Like, once a week. I feel like I barely see you anymore. And now you're forgetting about your art assignments, and you aren't drawing. That's not like you, Maddie." Before I could come up with an explanation for her statement, she continued. "And now you have a whole new crowd of friends. It's like I'm not even your best friend anymore."

My feet remained planted in place, but it felt like every word she threw at me made the space between us grow larger. "New friends? You mean Aaron? We've been friends for a long time."

Alaina's shoulders dropped. "It's not just Aaron. You seem to invite Dani over more than you invite me to hang out with you. What happened to our after-school hang outs?"

"I have cheerleading practice after school. You know that." I said the words like they'd make it all better, but they only felt empty.

She shook her head. "That's what I mean. You never wanted to be a cheerleader before, and now you're all pompoms and rah rah rah."

I didn't bother correcting her on the proper term for "pompons," but I did slowly slide them behind my back like I'd suddenly become self-conscious of them.

"Look, Alaina. I'm really sorry I missed your art night. I can go check out the artwork later this week. And besides, we still have dress shopping tomorrow for homecoming."

Alaina rolled her eyes in a way she'd never done to me before. It wasn't out of sarcasm but instead out of true annoyance. "Forget it. I don't want to go dress shopping with you anymore." She grabbed her purse and slid around the couch to the front door.

I couldn't bring myself to move from my spot at the bottom of the stairs, but I still managed to speak. "Alaina, please—"

She cut me off. "Just don't, Maddie. You've completely

changed, and I want the old Maddie back. Let me know when you find her." She flung the front door open, but before she made it outside, she paused and turned back to me. "You should have listened to me to begin with. I knew Aaron would be bad for you."

I didn't chase after her like I wanted to. I didn't try to reason with her. All I could do was stare dumbfounded after her.

Was this what it all came down to? Choosing between my boyfriend and my best friend? I didn't think I could make that kind of decision.

CHAPTER 13

LOGAN

After missing dress shopping with Alaina, thanks to Logan's surprise date, I didn't know what else to do but raid my sisters' closets the following week for an appropriate homecoming dress. I found three that could work.

The first was one of Kayla's dresses that had gold sparkles on top with a short golden skirt. When I couldn't manage to get the zipper up all the way, I tossed that one aside. Kayla had always been slimmer than me, so that was no surprise.

The second was a blue spaghetti strap dress of Amy's, but the skirt was so short that I was afraid I'd flash everyone. I threw that dress on top of the gold one on my bed and prayed the final dress would fit.

I'd found the last one in Amy's closet and held it out in front of me. It was strapless, but at least the skirt seemed a little longer than the blue one. The way the pink and purple fabric blended made the dress shimmer. I pulled it on and zipped it up before turning to the mirror. Once I did, I drew in a reflexive breath. It was *perfect*. It hugged my body just right, and the beading on the bodice was an attractive touch. I couldn't wait to see what Logan thought of it. I let an involuntary grin break across my face when I slid into my desk chair and let thoughts of Logan consume me. Sure, I was still feeling bad about missing dress shopping with Alaina, but at least the thought of going to the homecoming dance with Logan left me with a sense of comfort.

After pulling myself from my thoughts, I stripped off the pink and purple dress and hung it in my own closet before slipping on my pajamas. I threw the blue and gold dresses on their hangers and placed them back in my sisters' respective bedrooms.

When I returned to my own room, I sunk onto my bed and pulled the covers over me. I checked my phone before completely turning in for the night. That's when I noticed a text from Alaina. At least she wasn't so mad about missing dress shopping that she'd stopped talking to me, but every time I saw her name pop up on my notifications, a pang of guilt hit me. I swallowed the guilt and set my phone aside, praying we'd have enough fun at the dance that she'd forget about my recent behavior and forgive me. I fell asleep that night daydreaming about the upcoming dance.

Wednesday was pajama day at school, so I didn't bother changing into something new for the day. I donned my usual sneakers because I didn't have any decent slippers to wear, but I remained in my purple plaid pajama pants and white t-shirt. I applied a small amount of makeup and twisted my hair into a long braid that ran down my right shoulder. When I entered the school, it looked like all the students had arrived for a huge slumber party.

"Cute pajama pants," Emily told me when I found our group by our lockers.

"Thanks." I eyed her outfit. She wore pink flannel bottoms with a matching top, and her blond hair was fashioned into two matching braids, one on either side of her head. "Yours are cute, too."

I looked back up at my friends. Alaina gave me a smile, which told me that she was starting to forgive me for how I'd been acting lately. I opened my mouth to ask where Logan was, but before I could get a word out, I sensed the heat of his body behind me. My pulse quickened, and I turned to him in excitement. Before I could tell my body to simmer down, my arms flung around his neck. At least I had enough self-control to realize what I was doing a second later, and I managed to refrain from planting a kiss on his lips.

"Happy to see me?" he joked with a smile.

I drew away from him and stared into the beautiful blue eyes behind his glasses. The rest of our friends talked amongst themselves, and it nearly felt like we were alone. "I'm always happy to see you."

A rush of red rose to his cheeks. "I'm always happy to see you, too."

"Walk me to my locker?" I suggested.

As we walked, I checked out Logan's pajamas. His were blue plaid. "Hey, we almost match," I pointed out.

He gazed down at my pants, but the way he eyed them made me think he was checking out more than the fabric. "Indeed, we do. Hey, you aren't busy after school for any reason, are you?"

We reached my locker, and I spun the combination to

open it. I glanced back at him while I shoved my bag inside. "I'm not busy. Did you have something in mind?"

He raked his fingers through the ends of his hair. "I thought maybe we could hang out. How about another music lesson?"

I turned back to him with my textbook and notebook for first period in my arms. All I wanted to do was take a step closer to him, to touch him, but I knew I couldn't show my affection here with so many people around. I reflexively reached up to tuck a strand of hair behind my ear. There was nothing there since it was all in my braid. I let my hand fall to my side. "I think that sounds like a good idea." The warning bell rang just then. "I'll see you later."

I pulled out my sketchbook during first period and flipped to a new page. We had another sketch due this Friday like normal, and I wasn't going to forget this time. It was easy enough to get away with drawing during class because most of my teachers didn't notice. After the morning announcements finished, I began sketching the outline of fingers curled around the neck of a guitar—Logan's fingers around his guitar, Lucy. I didn't get very far on my drawing by the end of the period, but at least I had a start.

I brought my sketchbook with me to choir and showed Logan the drawing I was working on. I'd managed to add some shading since first period.

"That's amazing," he told me with a genuine smile.

Emily leaned toward me to take a peek. "Wow, Maddie. Yours and Alaina's artistic skills never cease to amaze me."

My face heated at the compliments. "Thanks, guys."

The room fell silent when the bell rang.

"Tenors at the piano, please," our instructor called.

Logan left my side to work on a section of song the tenors were having trouble with. I turned back to my sketchbook and added texture to Logan's fingers while Emily chatted about the upcoming play auditions next to me.

"Ready for that music lesson?" Logan asked after class.

I flipped my sketchbook closed and met his gaze with a smile. "Yeah. I'll meet you in the practice room. I'm going to go drop off my sketchbook and pencils in my locker and pick up my bag."

"Hurry back."

I glanced at him on my way out of the room to see that a grin had formed across his face. "Can't manage a few minutes without me?"

"You know I can't." His smile grew as he played along.

I didn't realize I was beaming until I reached the hall my locker stood in and noticed the crowd of other students. My expression reverted to normal as I hurried past them. I fumbled around inside my locker for a minute to gather my homework. Once organized inside my bag, I slung it over my shoulder so I didn't have to make another trip after Logan's music lesson.

I clicked my locker shut. When I looked up, I noticed I was alone. It usually didn't take more than two minutes for everyone to escape the building, so I wasn't surprised. What shocked me was when a hand gripped my wrist on my way back to the choir room. My heart leapt at the touch. I spun to face my assailant. My pulse slowed when I realized it was only Aaron, but a split second later, the pitter patter of my heart returned at full force. His eyes already told me what he wanted to say, and I didn't care to hear any of it.

"Don't," I insisted before he had a chance to speak. I turned my back to him and headed in the direction I was going before he interrupted me.

"Don't what?" he feigned, falling into step beside me.

"Don't say what you want to say."

I stared straight ahead. I didn't have to look at him to know an amused smile had formed across his face. It was evident in his tone.

"And what is it that I want to say?"

My lips pressed into a thin line. "Don't play dumb with me, Aaron."

He sighed beside me and then quickened his pace until he blocked my path. "Fine. I admit it. I was going to say something again, but if you'd actually listen to me, then maybe you'd see that I'm right, that you made the wrong choice."

I stubbornly crossed my arms over my chest and stared him dead in the eye. "It's insulting, Aaron. I shouldn't have to listen to you insult my choices and my boyfriend."

His lips twitched like he was trying to hold back a smile. "I'm not insulting Logan. He's a great guy. He's just not the guy for you."

"You're wrong." I attempted to push past him with the force of my elbow, but he side-stepped in front of me. The surface of my skin heated in anger. Where did he get the idea that he had the right to do this to me, to insult me and block my path? And what would it take for him to let me go on my way?

I planted my feet and crossed my arms over my chest for a second time. Fine. If letting him talk would get rid of him, then that was the only choice I had, but it wasn't going to end well for him. There was nothing he could say to change my mind.

"Fine, Aaron. Talk."

He blinked a few times as if shocked that I'd given him the chance to explain himself. After a long moment where he didn't speak, I figured he was just going to stand there like a mute fool for the next few minutes. I didn't have the time for that, but as soon as my body twitched to move past him, he spoke to stop me.

"It's just… I can't stop thinking about you." He raked his fingers through his hair like he didn't know what else to do with his hands. "Every time I see you with him, it's like…" His voice trailed off.

"Like?" I prompted. The urge to tap my foot impatiently overcame me, but I resisted.

Aaron scanned the empty hall, avoiding my gaze. "It's just wrong."

I narrowed my eyes at him. "Wrong for who?" *For him, not for me, but there's nothing I can do to fix that. If he really loved me, he would let me be happy with Logan.*

He finally looked at me. "For everyone, Maddie."

Clearly, he wasn't going to back down.

"Aaron," I stated sternly. "You asked me to make a choice. You said whoever I didn't choose would move on. I made a choice. Now you have to move on."

His shoulders dropped. "I know I said that, but I changed my mind. Just like you can change yours."

My voice rose slightly. "And what makes you think you'd be any better for me than Logan is? Because you love me? Well, guess what. Logan loves me, too."

I said the words, but in the same moment, I realized that Logan never actually told me he loved me. But he had to, right?

Aaron's jaw tensed. "I can't put it into words, Maddie. I

just know you belong right here," he pointed to his heart, "with me."

A sinking sensation entered my chest. I hated knowing I was the one who broke his heart, but it wasn't fair that he was trying to break mine, either. The air between us grew heavy in the silence that followed.

Aaron's whisper broke through the quietness. "I know there's a piece of you that still loves me, too."

And then that space between us, the one that held the heavy air, vanished. Aaron's body pressed against mine, and his arms wrapped around me in an embrace I couldn't wiggle free from. His lips met mine in a soft, gentle encounter.

And that's when a fire ignited in my body. Though his lips were on mine for only a split second, the encounter transported my mind elsewhere, outside of the school hall I knew I was still standing in. In my vision, I lay on the ground, and a soft blue hue filled the space. Somehow, I knew I was lying under a sheet fort Aaron and I had built like when we were kids. His body hovered above me, his lips connecting with mine. My heart slammed against my rib cage, and his sweet kiss sent shivers of exhilaration up and down my spine.

Pulling my attention back to the school hallway, I didn't allow myself the time to consider what it all meant. The images I was seeing couldn't be anything but shock, could they? I wiggled my arms to his chest and pushed against him as hard as I could. The fire I'd felt just moments before fizzled to nothing.

Aaron stumbled back and braced himself against someone else's locker. Despite the shove I'd given him, he beamed so much that his dimple appeared.

I stared at him wide eyed, unable to speak.

"*That's* what it's like to love me, Maddie."

I blinked several times, still trying to process what had just occurred. "I—I have to go. Logan's waiting for me."

I raced off toward the choir room. When I entered it, I finally slowed my pace. A sigh of relief escaped my lungs when I realized Aaron hadn't chased after me. After a moment to let my heart rate slow, I finally took the time to reflect back on Aaron's kiss. It was so warm, inviting, and passionate. It was like…

What am I thinking!?

I forced my breath to slow further.

Logan! Logan is the guy I want to be with. Aaron completely stepped out of line. That didn't just happen, did it? Can I at least pretend it didn't happen?

I took one final calming breath to mask my shock before entering the practice room to join Logan. I only prayed he couldn't read me and see what I was hiding from him.

CHAPTER 14

AARON

After Alaina told me she didn't want to go dress shopping with me anymore, I sulked around the house wondering what I was going to do about everything. First of all, I had to get Alaina to forgive me, but she wouldn't return any of my texts over the weekend. Then there was the issue of finding a dress to wear to the homecoming dance. Whether Alaina was upset at me or not, I wasn't going to miss my special night with Aaron.

I didn't bother texting Emily and Holly to go shopping with me because I knew I didn't deserve anyone's sympathy for how I'd made Alaina feel. Besides, I didn't have a ton of money for a dress anyway. It was only when I was contemplating what to do that I realized I had a stash of dresses at my fingertips all along. I raided my sisters' closets and found three contenders.

The first and second dresses were no good, so I was surprised when I slipped on the final dress and it fit me like a glove. The pink and purple fabric shimmered under the light.

I stared at myself in the mirror to admire the dress, but disappointment soon caught up with me. I sighed and stripped it off before hanging it in my closet. Would Alaina forgive me by the time the dance rolled around? Would I have any fun without her?

By Thursday, I still didn't have an answer. I'd sat at Aaron's table at lunch all week, and Alaina had remained mostly quiet during art class. It was like we were both waiting for the other to say something first. When I spotted Alaina near her locker that morning, I decided I should be the one to finally speak up.

"Alaina?"

She turned her back on her open locker to face me. It was crazy hair day at school today, so one side of her hair was secured into a piggy tail, and the other was twisted into a braid. Mine was fashioned in the same way, and for a moment, I focused on how much we thought alike, like we were still best friends. Weren't we?

"Yeah?" Her tone came out completely neutral, so I couldn't tell what she was thinking.

I hadn't planned what to say to her, but after a split second of silence, I knew I had to spit out something. I settled on the first friendly thought that came to mind. "Do you want to sit together at lunch today?"

A twitch of a smile hit her lips, and her voice came out soft, almost inviting. "I'd like that."

I walked away feeling victorious.

"I told Alaina I'd sit by her at lunch today," I mentioned to Aaron when I met up with him at his locker.

He shrugged. "Sounds good."

"Really?" I asked hopefully.

He draped his arm around me as he walked me over to my locker. "Well, I know that whole thing that happened last weekend has been bothering you. You've been complaining about it all week."

"I have?" I furrowed my brow, but looking back on it, I realized I had talked to Aaron a lot about it recently. I quickly let the subject drop. "So, your hair…"

Aaron didn't have a ton of hair to work with for crazy hair day, but what he did have he'd fashioned into small spikes secured with tiny colorful hairbands.

He touched the top of his spikes. "Yeah, it was my mom's idea. I know it's hard to believe, but these are actually her elastics." I glanced back at him to see a huge grin spread across his face.

I laughed. "Strange. I really would have thought they were yours."

He responded with a lighthearted shove.

I couldn't explain my excitement as lunch approached. It was like Alaina's acceptance of me sitting by her at lunch meant she'd forgiven me. I hadn't heard much from Logan this past week, but maybe he'd forgiven me, too. I hurried out of my last class before lunch and shoved my notebook in my locker. Before I took another step, I realized one of my shoes was untied. I bent to tie it. By the time I stood, everyone had already fled the halls to the lunchroom. I didn't bother hurrying since I knew I'd be at the end of the line anyway. It was only when I passed the choir room that something caught my eye.

Logan's blond hair moved from behind a window to one of the practice rooms. Though it was crazy hair day and he had more hair to work with than Aaron did, he'd left it natural. I paused briefly and wondered what he was up to. If he was hanging out in a practice room, did that mean he wouldn't be at our table at lunch today?

Before I could continue on toward the cafeteria, Logan's gaze lifted, and he noticed me. I hurried on my way, pretending I didn't see him, but it was no use. Our eyes had locked, and he knew I saw him.

"Maddie." He caught up with me far too quickly.

I put on a smile before turning back to him, hoping he'd appreciate the friendly gesture. "What's up, Logan? Are you headed to lunch?"

"I was going to in a minute, but I'm finishing up working on a song I was practicing during my study hall last period." He looked toward the ground for a moment and then back up at me. A light shade of red settled over his cheeks. "Do you want to hear it?"

For a moment, I couldn't believe he was asking me that, but I quickly relaxed when I realized his invitation was also a sign that he wanted to be friends again. He was no longer ignoring me, so that was a plus. Since I'd be at the end of the lunch line anyway, I figured I had a few moments to spare.

"Sure," I answered.

Logan led me into one of the practice rooms and clicked the door shut behind us. He lifted a guitar onto his lap while a proud smile crossed his face. "What do you think of her?"

"That's *your* guitar?" I asked, slightly surprised.

He plucked at the strings. "Yep. Just picked her up last week."

A sense of comfort washed over me in response to Logan's inviting tone. "That's pretty cool. So, what song were you practicing?"

His lips twitched like he was trying to hold back a smile. "An original."

My mouth dropped open slightly before forming into a smile. "That's awesome. I had no idea you were so talented."

He shrugged like it was no big deal. "Yeah, well, I've written a couple of songs."

"Cool. Let's hear it!" Sitting there with him made it feel almost like nothing had ever happened between us, like we'd never had a falling out. We eased back into being friends so easily.

Logan resituated himself in his seat. "Okay. This song is really important to me, and I wanted you to be the first to hear it."

"Me?"

He nodded. "The lyrics really mean a lot to me, and it's easier for me to express myself through song."

"Okay." Though I didn't know what his song was about, he had me intrigued.

Logan took a long, deep breath as if working up the courage to begin strumming. He paused for a moment, only long enough for me to catch his hesitation, before he closed his eyes, relaxed his shoulders, and strummed his first chord. He filled the entire room with a slow, beautiful tune. His posture changed until he sat slightly straighter in his seat. It was like now that he was playing, he didn't see any chance of backing out, and that gave him the confidence he needed to continue. He never opened his eyes, even when he began singing the lyrics.

I had my chance with you.
or so I thought.
But all you did
was cut me off.
We could have been
something great.
Just when I thought I had you there,
you turned away.

And now all that's left are
pieces of dreams.
They haunt me while I sleep,
but they keep me company.
And I still wonder:
Was I strong enough?
I still don't know.
I thought I'd let you go.
But you come back to me
in pieces of dreams.

As his tenor voice filled the practice room, my heart began to warm. The sound was so peaceful, so magical, and somehow, that tune found its way into my soul. It was like the song was composed just for me, like it was mine.

It was only when Logan's voice faded at the end of the chorus that I had a chance to reflect on what the words meant. I snapped back to reality. Just as Logan pulled in a deep breath to begin the second verse, I shot up in my chair.

"This song is about *me?*" I interrupted in a harsher tone than I intended.

Logan immediately stopped and placed his hand over the

strings of the guitar to mute the music. The magic in the room that was there just moments ago vanished in a heartbeat. Logan's sad blue eyes stared up at me as if to ask what he'd done wrong.

I wanted to scold him, to tell him how a minute ago it felt like we were getting back to being friends, and he'd ruined the moment by telling me how much he still thought about me. I was wrong to assume we'd made any progress.

But I didn't say any of that. I couldn't manage to force the words out of my throat. It was like a small piece of my heart had broken off and lodged itself in my airways. Water rose to my eyes, and the only thing I could think to do was reach for the door handle. My only choices were to stay and watch Logan's heart shatter again—thanks to me—or flee and pretend he'd never admitted his feelings to me.

I swallowed down the lump in my throat just long enough to sputter, "I—I have to go."

"Maddie, wait." Logan caught me before I could reach the hallway.

I whirled to face him. "This isn't fair, Logan!"

He took a step back like I'd slapped him.

I didn't waste a moment to clarify. "You guys told me that whoever I didn't choose would move on. Do you think this is easy for me to see you heartbroken? You're still my friend. I still *care*. But you can't just serenade me with Lucy and think that's *fair*. Why can't we just be *friends*? Why does there have to be all this 'pieces of dreams' crap? I like the days when we can goof off and wipe ice cream on each other's faces without it feeling all complicated. Why can't we go back to that? Why are my only choices being your girlfriend or not being anything at all? Why can't we just be friends?"

Logan cut in as soon as I took a moment to breathe. "Maddie, I'm sorry. I didn't realize you'd react like this. I wasn't trying to get you or anything. It's just how I feel, and I can't help that." He shoved his hands in his pockets and stared at the floor shyly. When I didn't say anything back, he spoke again. "And what do you mean about the ice cream food fight?"

I furrowed my brow at him. "You know. It was when we went out for ice cream. Your ice cream cone grazed my nose, and I got you back."

If possible, Logan shoved his hands into his pockets even deeper. "That never happened, Maddie. Not with us, anyway."

"What? Of course it did. It was just a couple of weeks ago…" My voice trailed off. Was it? We weren't even talking a couple of weeks ago.

"That must have been something with Aaron," Logan stated.

Well, Aaron and I *did* go get ice cream together. How was it that I remembered Logan was there, too?

His eyes dropped shyly again. "And I never told you the name of my guitar, either. How'd you know that?"

His gaze lifted, and I froze. How *did* I know that? An ill sensation twisted in my gut, and my throat closed up, preventing the response I didn't even have.

"Are you okay?" Logan asked with genuine concern.

I swallowed hard but could still barely answer. "Yeah, I—I think I might be getting sick. Excuse me."

When I fled, he didn't chase after me. Confusion followed me all the way to the lunchroom. I managed to make it just as the last few students filed through the line. I grabbed my lunch and then hurried to sit between Alaina and Aaron, all the while trying to shake off my encounter with Logan.

"What took you so long?" Aaron asked gently.

I almost didn't hear him, but a moment later, his question registered. "Me? Oh, my shoe was giving me troubles." At least that wasn't a lie. I turned back to my food and hoped my piggy tail concealed enough of my face that he couldn't tell I was hiding something from him.

CHAPTER 15
LOGAN

I spent Thursday and Friday doing my best not to think about Aaron at school, but every time I saw him in the halls or in class, the memory of our kiss found its way to the forefront of my mind. Eventually, it seemed to make a permanent home there.

It didn't help that I'd now had two semi-romantic dreams about Aaron. In one, we ran around the mall having a blast in the photo booth and on those small kiddie rides you pay a quarter or two to sway back and forth on. In the other, Aaron and I sat cuddled on my couch while we watched—well, mostly watched—a movie. The scary part was how vivid the dreams were.

I did my best not to look at him across the lunchroom on Friday, but it took all my willpower, so much that I didn't even engage in the conversation at lunch. The grip on my fork tightened. A sudden urge to stand in front of the entire lunchroom and scream at him overcame me.

How could you do this to me? I imagined myself yelling. *Don't you see what you've done? I can't enjoy time with my friends anymore because all I think about now is you and that kiss! I made up my mind. I chose Logan. And now I don't know how to feel. Why couldn't you just move on like you said you would? It would have been easier for everyone!*

Of course, I refrained myself from confronting him.

I knew the best thing was to be honest with Logan and tell him about the kiss. After all, it's not like I kissed Aaron back, was it? Except, I still couldn't bring myself to mention it to anyone. It was like if I didn't talk about it, it didn't happen. Luckily, Aaron hadn't tried to talk to me since. I wondered if that meant he was giving up on me or if it just meant he thought giving me distance was the next step in winning me over.

Well, it won't work! I thought angrily on my way to dump my tray.

In art, Alaina dropped her sketchbook next to me on our table, startling me out of my daze. I quickly slammed my own sketchbook closed so she wouldn't see the drawing of Aaron I'd just been staring at. I'd sketched it last night and had nearly finished it before I really knew what I was drawing.

"What's up?" Alaina slid into her seat beside me before the bell rang.

"Oh—uh." I shrugged. "Nothing."

She scooted her chair closer to me. "Something's clearly bothering you. You've been acting strange since yesterday. You didn't say a word at lunch, and you hardly ate your lasagna."

Crap. She noticed. I hope Logan didn't.

"I've just been tired," I answered vaguely.

She eyed me suspiciously. "You owe me a real explanation."

"I do not!" I answered too quickly.

"Well, you owe me something for ditching out of dress shopping last weekend."

Ouch. That stung so much that I had to hold back a wince. I glanced around at my classmates to stall. The bell for class rang before I could answer. I didn't have the time to explain, and I didn't want anyone else to overhear. Still, Alaina was right. I owed her something.

"Fine, but not now. Come over after school, and we can hang out before the homecoming game."

Her eyes brightened. "Ooh, maybe we could have a sleepover afterward and then I can hang out until the dance tomorrow. We can get ready for it together."

I smiled back at her. "That sounds like a lot of fun."

"Spill," Alaina demanded. She dropped her bag onto my bed next to Parrot, who was sleeping and didn't even acknowledge we were there. "What's been up with you the past couple of days?"

I shut my bedroom door even though my parents weren't home. My cheeks grew hot as I sank into my desk chair and stared down at Logan's bracelet around my wrist. In the next moment, a guilty sensation hit my gut. I shrugged without meeting Alaina's gaze. I knew I'd end up admitting the truth to her, but I hadn't yet found the courage. "Well, first of all, you've been mad at me all week."

I caught Alaina's head drop from out of the corner of my eye. "Yeah, I guess, but you deserved it."

"I did," I admitted sheepishly, "but I still don't like knowing you're mad at me. I thought about what you said."

"Which thing I said?"

I leaned down to reach into my bag for my sketchbook. "About how I was changing myself for Logan. I've been drawing more. See?" I flipped to the drawing of Logan's hand on his guitar and set the book next to her on my comforter.

Alaina's brows shot up. "Wow. That's really good. I mean, your drawings are always good, but..." She paused to inspect the drawing. "This one has so much *detail.*" She slowly flipped the pages through the next few drawings, eyeing each of them carefully.

Before she reached the latest one of Aaron, I pulled the sketchbook back and stuffed it in my bag. "See? I'm still the same old Maddie. I might even be better now." I said the words, but they didn't feel true.

Alaina laughed, a sound that told me she'd forgiven me. "I'm fine now. I promise. I just want to go to the homecoming dance with you tomorrow without being mad at each other."

I relaxed. "Do you want to see my dress? I stole one of Amy's. It's really pretty." Without waiting for an answer, I stood and headed to my closet. When I turned around with the dress in hand, Alaina was frowning. "What?"

"It is pretty, but whatever has been happening the past couple of days has nothing to do with me or the dress. Did something happen between you and Logan?"

My words came out too fast for my own liking. "What? Why would you think that?"

"You didn't answer the question," she accused.

I sighed and turned to place the dress back in my closet. Before answering, I sank onto my bed opposite her. "No, nothing happened between me and Logan." I bit my lip nervously, and my pulse quickened. Alaina was my best friend, and I'd never held something from her for so long. I took a deep breath before working up enough courage to tell her the truth. My heart hammered as the confession tumbled out of my mouth. "But something happened between me and Aaron."

"What?" she practically shouted. "What kind of something?"

My gaze locked on the lavender lampshade next to my bed. I couldn't look her in the eyes. "Aaron kissed me."

Her jaw dropped. "Oh my gosh. That sleaze ball." She eyed me to assess my reaction, but my expression didn't change. "Or not."

I plopped onto my back on the bed, and my eyes turned up to the ceiling. Finally, Parrot noticed and hopped onto the floor. He proceeded to crawl under the bed.

"I don't know," I complained. "At first, I thought the same thing. How could he think he had any right to do that?"

Alaina lowered herself next to me and propped her head up on one elbow. "Well, did you kiss him back?"

I went quiet for a beat and then spoke in a whisper. "I can't remember." My words hung in the air for several seconds.

Thankfully, Alaina eased the awkwardness. "You know what I think?" She didn't wait for an answer before she continued. "I think you need a break from these guys. *Both* of them."

Both of them? I nearly cried out as if the thought was completely ludicrous, but I shut my jaw tight. I didn't think an outburst like that would help.

"Let's be honest," Alaina continued. "Nothing has been the same since you made your decision. I still stand by what I said last weekend. You've been changing yourself for Logan, and I don't think it's healthy."

"So, what?" I asked, never tearing my gaze from the ceiling

above me. "I should just not choose either of them? I should just be alone for the rest of my life?"

"Not the rest of your life. But for now, yeah. That's exactly what I think."

I finally swiveled my head to look at her, but I couldn't bring myself to agree nor disagree.

CHAPTER 16

AARON

By Friday morning, I had a stronger sense of what Logan meant by "you come back to me in pieces of dreams." Thursday night, I'd dreamt that Logan took me out to a waterfall to have a picnic, and we spent hours cuddled in each other's arms just staring at the sky. It's crazy how it could feel I'd lived an entire day in what must have been just a few minutes of dreaming.

That morning, I threw my hair into a messy bun and dressed in my cheerleading uniform since it was school spirit dress up day. I couldn't remember the last time I'd worn my hair up, since Aaron liked it down, but somehow, it seemed like it suited me today.

I did my best to avoid Logan in the hall that morning, but he caught my eye as I passed by. I shyly turned away, but that didn't quiet the tune to his song that played through my head. *Why did I put my hair up this morning?* I wondered to myself while wishing I had something to conceal my face at the moment. As I approached Aaron's locker, I could still feel

Logan's eyes on the back of my head. I forced myself to ignore it.

"Some people take this school spirit thing way too seriously," I joked to Aaron once I reached him. I glanced around the hall and noticed several girls in blue and white tutu skirts and tall heels.

"Well, the guys need a reason to play well." He eyed one of the girls in a tutu up and down in jest.

I swatted at him playfully. "You mean your team only plays well when there are pretty girls in the audience?"

"Don't forget about the pretty girls on the cheerleading squad." He beamed.

I smiled back as we headed to my locker. Somehow, even as I bent down at my locker and fixed my gaze on my notebooks, I could feel Logan approaching. The sensation of him watching me intensified. I glanced up just as he passed me. Our eyes locked for a split second, and my heart skipped a beat. Aaron didn't seem to notice my discomfort. I drew in a breath of courage and then stood holding my notebook.

"Walk me to class?" I suggested.

Aaron took my hand and agreed.

At lunch, I couldn't help but glance at Logan every now and then. Aaron and I had compromised and joined my friends' table again. Logan actually engaged in the conversation today, which seemed strange. Did that mean he was getting over things, or did his statements from the day before still stand?

"I have to use the bathroom," Alaina stated after we finished our food.

"Me, too," Holly agreed.

"And me," Emily joined in.

I glanced up at the three of them. Was there some party happening in the girls' bathroom I didn't know about? Emily subtly widened her eyes at me, a message that I should join them.

"Me, four."

I heard the guys chuckle as we all walked away. "Why do girls always have to go to the bathroom in groups?" Blake asked. I didn't hear a response as we distanced ourselves from the table.

"So, what's with the secret party in the bathroom?" I asked as soon as the door swung shut behind us.

All three of my friends turned to stare at me.

"What?" I asked innocently. I didn't have anything to be guilty about, did I?

Holly spoke with a smile on her face. "What's with you and Logan?"

Emily wiggled her blond eyebrows, and Alaina leaned against the bathroom counter with an amused expression on her face.

"Me and Logan?" I asked, honestly confused. "What are you talking about?"

Holly pushed her dark curls out of her face. "Well, Logan hinted…"

My teeth gritted. What was Logan saying about me?

"Yeah," Alaina said. "While you and Aaron were still in line, Jordan asked Logan if he had a date for the dance. He said something about he hoped, and then he looked at you."

"What?" I nearly shouted. I couldn't believe the nerve of that guy. "Nothing is happening between us! I'm going to the dance with Aaron. Why would he say something like that?"

"Well." Emily dragged out the word and glanced around at

the rest of us. "He did share the lyrics of his song with me yesterday in choir."

"Oh my gosh!" I buried my face in my hands. How could Logan think he still had a chance with me? He didn't. At least, that's what I told myself. I wasn't entirely sure after hearing his song yesterday.

"Song?" Alaina asked Emily. "You didn't mention a song."

"She told me," Holly said proudly. "Something about… what was it? He dreams about Maddie and still loves her and…"

"Yeah, kind of," Emily explained. "It was about how he was trying to get over her but couldn't…"

Their voices faded into the background while a wave of heat overcame me. I still hadn't dropped my hands from my face, but I leaned my hip against the corner of the counter to steady myself. Sure, Logan's song was beautiful, he had magnificent eyes, and I felt comfortable around him, but Aaron was the one I chose. Still, it would be nice to give him a chance, to really see what it would feel like to lie in his arms for hours on end, to taste his kiss, to—

I quickly shut down that thought and dropped my hands. My attention focused back on the conversation.

"That sounds sweet," Alaina said. She turned to me. "I told you Logan was a good guy. I mean, the guy wrote a *song* for you. If that's not romantic, then I don't know what—"

"Aaron," I said too loudly, cutting her off. I didn't even want to think about Logan right now. When I did, it was like I forgot all about Aaron and had to say his name just to remember he existed.

All three of my friends stared at me, shocked by my outburst.

"Aaron is romantic," I stated, more for myself than for

them. "He knows me. He's funny. We get along." But at the same time, I got along with Logan just fine. He was talented and sweet, and he really cared about me. "Aaron," I said again to reassure myself that his name felt like the right one on my tongue. "I don't know why Logan thinks a *song* is going to change my mind. And you can tell him that."

And then I stormed out of the bathroom. I didn't know where else to go, so I headed to my locker. We weren't really supposed to be out of the cafeteria during lunch period, but the bell would ring shortly, so I didn't think anyone would notice. When I reached my locker, I opened it and fell to my knees. For a moment, I just stared ahead. Then I pulled Aaron's necklace away from my chest to examine it.

Aaron. I chose Aaron. Here's the proof.

I let the necklace go so that it swung freely from my neck. The weight felt good, felt *right*, like it was the only thing I needed to remind me of where I belonged. So why did it feel like something was missing from my wrist?

Aaron picked me up on the way to the homecoming game that night. "Ready to cheer really hard for me?"

"Well, you need a reason to play well," I joked, repeating the words he'd said earlier.

He glanced at me for a split second like he didn't know what I was talking about, and then he relaxed. "It helps."

We reached the field, but he didn't get out of the car right away. Instead, he leaned over toward me. It took me a second to realize I had pulled away from his kiss. As soon as I noticed, I consciously closed the distance between us. He left a light kiss on my lips, but for some reason, it didn't seem as warm as usual.

"Good luck tonight," I told him once he'd pulled away.

"Thanks. You, too."

When I reached the sidelines, I immediately headed over to Dani.

"Are you as pumped about this game as I am?" she asked excitedly.

I shot her a smile but didn't answer. Instead, I scanned the crowd. Almost everyone dressed in blue and white, and it seemed like the whole student body had arrived to cheer on the Eagles.

Dani didn't waste a second pointing out the huge crowd. "I know the crowd is bigger tonight than usual, but we've all worked really hard on our stunts and our cheers. You'll all do fine. If you get nervous, just picture the audience in their underwear."

Dani laughed like it was a ridiculous suggestion. Surprisingly, though, the thought actually helped me relax. When I eyed the crowd and spotted Logan near the pep band, I lost my conscious grip on my imagination.

Stop it! I told myself. I did *not* need to be imagining those things.

"Thanks a lot, Dani." I rolled my eyes to ease my mood. It helped.

After the Eagle's victory, I hugged Aaron tight when he found me on the sidelines. "You did great tonight!"

He shrugged. "I missed that first field goal, but at least we won."

Somehow, I didn't catch the field goal he'd missed. We must have been facing the crowd in a cheer or I didn't recognize him compared to all his other teammates in blue and white jerseys. *But I should have at least recognized his number*, I thought.

"Yeah," I said. "At least you won."

"Any chance you want to hang out tonight?"

Before I could answer, an involuntary yawn escaped my lungs.

"Ah, I see," he joked. "You need your beauty rest before the dance tomorrow night."

I smiled shyly. "Something like that."

Aaron dropped me off at home, but it was only after I stripped off my cheerleading uniform and sank down into bed that I realized I'd rushed into the house so fast that I forgot to give him a kiss.

Sighing, I rolled over and reached for my purse on the floor. I pulled it up next to me on the bed and dug through the outside pocket until my fingers grazed the piece of paper I was looking for. Holding the photograph above me, I stared at each pose Aaron and I had taken at the photo booth in the mall. I didn't know why I felt the need to relive that moment in my mind. I guess I thought that if I could remind myself how much fun we had together, I'd feel that giddiness in my chest again. Only, that's not what I felt. As I stared at the pictures, the only thing I could think was what it would be like if Logan was in those images instead of Aaron.

"What's happening to you, Maddie?" I questioned myself out loud. Quickly realizing how crazy I sounded talking to myself, I turned my discussion inward. *Get a grip, girl!* Another voice quickly countered, *I have a grip.* I didn't think I believed myself.

CHAPTER 17
LOGAN

I awoke Saturday morning on my living room couch. It took me a moment to recall why I wasn't sleeping in my own bed, and then I remembered that Alaina and I had crashed in the living room after the homecoming game the previous night. The game where I spent more time watching Aaron on the field than holding my boyfriend's hand in the stands.

I quickly shook off the memory. I'd held Logan's hand, hadn't I? *Yeah, I did,* I told myself, remembering at least one instance where our hands were entwined when he wasn't playing his saxophone.

I managed to pull my eyes open completely, and I glanced over at Alaina on the other couch. It was shorter than the one I was lying on, so she had her knees pulled up to fit.

Her eyes flittered open. "Good morning." Her voice came out groggy. She cleared her throat and tried again. This time, it came out clear. "Good morning."

"So, are you excited?" I asked with a smile.

She pushed herself to a seated position. "It's just a dance."

She couldn't hide her own grin. "But yeah, I'm excited. Jordan is going to love my dress. Hey, what time is it? We should get Emily and Holly over here so we can get ready together." She reached for her phone in her purse on the floor. "I'll text them."

"Sounds good." I stood and headed to the kitchen to grab myself a bowl of cereal, even though it was closer to lunch time than breakfast time.

It wasn't long before Emily and Holly arrived with a total of six bags of makeup and hair supplies. Since it was still early, though, we decided to kill some time with a card game. We all took a spot on the floor around the coffee table.

Alaina poked at her phone while Holly dealt the cards. A smile grew across her face while she stared down at the screen. "Hey, guys. Guess whose painting came in second place at the community art night?"

I immediately leaned over to view her screen. "You did? Really?"

The wide grin remained plastered on her face. "I know it's all just for fun, but it feels like an honor."

I scanned the web page she'd pulled up to see the picture of a flower garden had come in first and Alana's painting was second. I personally would have given her first.

"Congrats," I said, settling back into my spot and picking up my cards. Emily and Holly gave her their own congratulations before we began the game.

Eventually, Emily suggested we start getting ready. "Who wants to be my first torture victim?" she asked while holding up her curling iron.

"You're not getting that thing near me." Alaina backed away. She claimed her stick-straight hair was due to never using damaging products or heat on it. She always said she'd like to keep it that way.

Emily snapped her curling iron in my direction.

I sighed. "I will."

I spent the next few hours seated in front of my mirror while Emily curled my dark hair into spirals. Holly turned on Pandora and worked on taming her own natural curls, and Alaina sat on my bed petting Parrot while we all chatted. Once Emily locked my hair in place with practically a full bottle of hair spray, she took my place at the mirror to curl her own hair. I proceeded to add my makeup from beside her.

Eventually, we were all dolled up. Emily must have taken a million selfies of us all before Alaina announced it was almost time to go. I was just slipping on a pair of Kayla's strappy high heels when the doorbell rang.

"Were all the guys coming together?" I asked Emily, who had been the one to take the reins on the plans for the night. Somehow, I'd tuned out the discussion at lunch and forgot.

"Yep," she answered, bouncing her blond curls in her hand for the last time. "They should all be here. Blake's borrowing his mom's van so that we all fit."

We all hurried downstairs to meet the guys on my front steps. I opened the door to find Jordan standing behind it. He looked past me toward Alaina, who wore a short green dress with cap sleeves and had a matching green headband in her hair.

"You ladies ready?" Jordan asked without ever taking his eyes off Alaina.

"We sure are," I answered back. "Let me just say goodbye to my parents."

Before leaving, I popped into the kitchen, where my mom was putting away dishes from the dish washer. "We're leaving now," I told her as I placed a quick kiss on her cheek. "I'll see you later tonight."

"Okay, but did you and your friends want any pictures before you leave?"

I shrugged. "It's not a big deal. Emily got enough of us upstairs, and we'll get plenty at the dance."

"Okay, have fun," she told me.

Before I reached the front door, I leaned into my dad's office to tell him I was leaving.

"Have fun," he told me without looking up from his computer. "Text us if you're going to be out past midnight."

"I will. Bye, Dad."

"Bye."

I hurried outside to the van and climbed in behind my friends.

Logan greeted me with a smile. "You look great, Maddie."

"Thanks," I told him with sincerity as he kissed my check. My heart fluttered in response. *See?* I told myself. *I still love Logan. Aaron's kiss meant nothing.*

I glanced around the van. Blake was driving, and Holly sat in the passenger seat since they were going to the dance together "as friends." Alaina and Jordan sat in the seat in front of me, his arm draped around hers. Emily sat in the back by Logan and me. She was attending the dance with a guy she knew from choir, but he was supposed to meet us at the café for dinner before the dance. Then she'd ride with him to the dance later. That part I remembered.

I slid my hand into Logan's and held it all the way through dinner. The tension I'd been holding in my shoulders for the past few days eased. By the end of dinner, a sense of comfort settled over me, and I knew that it didn't matter how many times Aaron tried to win me over. I'd always choose Logan.

By the time we arrived at the high school gymnasium, there was already a good number of people there. Several people jumped up and down on the dance floor, but for the most part, people remained seated at tables lining the gym walls. Each round table was cloaked in either a blue or white tablecloth for the school colors. They matched the streamers hanging from the ceiling. White Christmas lights twinkled above us, giving the dim room a romantic hue. Our group ventured over to an empty table to claim it.

"Ugh," Emily complained. "What's the point of coming to a dance if you don't even dance? Look, the homecoming court isn't even dancing. Come on, Dustin," she grabbed onto her date's hand, "let's show these losers what real dancing looks like." She glanced back at us with a teasing smile.

Jordan shot her a challenging glare while he stripped off his jacket and followed after her. "I'll show her a thing or two about dancing." Holly and Blake ran off to join him.

I giggled as my friends hit the dance floor and began a sort of dance battle. Glancing over at Alaina, I noticed she beamed while she stared after Jordan.

She noticed my gaze and looked at me. "Well, he didn't take those dance classes for nothing."

When she went back to watching Jordan, I turned to Logan beside me, whose hand was still in my own. "Are you going to dance?"

He gave a shy smile that didn't come off as genuine. "I prefer to keep my feet grounded when I perform. But I'll save all the slow songs for you."

My heart gave another nervous flutter in my chest. "Deal."

I glanced back toward the dance floor to see that my friends, namely Jordan, were taking up the spotlight. Then I noticed Aaron had joined the dance floor as well. He appeared to be alone, but his dance moves weren't half bad.

He's so confident, I thought to myself in admiration. A split second later, I realized where my thoughts were going. I quickly looked back toward Logan to take my mind off Aaron.

When the first slow song came on, Logan pulled me up from my chair. "Ready for that first dance?" he asked.

My heart felt as if it were floating in my chest. Our first dance together! "Yes," I told him, but it came out softer than I intended.

He led me to the dance floor and slowly spun me around until I stopped in his embrace. "You look so beautiful tonight. Did you know that?"

I couldn't control the blush that rose to my cheeks, but all I could think to say was, "Emily did my hair."

"It looks nice," he said before pulling me close.

I wrapped my arms tighter around his neck and swayed with him to the music. He didn't say anything again, and neither did I. We simply enjoyed the thrill of being in each other's arms.

This, I thought to myself. *This is where I'm supposed to be.* As if I needed the extra reassurance, I leaned in and pressed my lips to his. I didn't worry about the other students or if the chaperones would spot us. Right now, it was just about Logan and how I felt about him. Yet when I pulled away, I didn't feel any different. His kiss didn't change the fact that when I stared across the room toward Aaron, my heart warmed in a way that it didn't with Logan. Though when I looked back at him, I melted.

It made no sense!

"You okay?" Logan asked. The distress must have been evident on my face.

I tried to ignore my own internal battle, but it did no good. "Let's go sit back down." I purposely didn't answer his question, but he agreed without pushing it.

We sat in silence for the next couple of songs. Logan attempted to ease the situation by offering to get us drinks.

I gave him a forced smile. "Sure."

"Ugh, look at them." Alaina gestured to the dance floor once Logan stood and walked away. "I wish I could dance."

"You should," I encouraged. "You should go dance with them. I'm sure Jordan would love to dance with you."

She tucked a strand of brunette hair behind her ear, but it didn't stay. "We danced during the slow song. He's just so good. I feel like I'd make a fool out of myself dancing next to him."

I followed her gaze and watched Jordan twirl on the dance floor. He definitely had talent.

"I'll go if you go," she promised.

A surge of adrenaline shot through my veins. Me? Dance? "Alaina, I don't—"

"Please?" She raised her eyebrows as if that would help her argument.

I sighed. It helped a little. "Fine."

I stood with her and joined my friends on the dance floor. Mostly, I just jumped up and down near my friends. Most of our eyes were locked on Jordan's dance moves and Blake's overly confident attempts at looking hot.

Holly laughed from beside me. "Can you believe I agreed to be his date?" She gestured toward Blake. "You wouldn't believe this, but he's actually okay at slow dancing."

I shot her back a smile because I wasn't sure what to say,

and it was hard to hear above the music anyway. It seemed like only a minute since Alaina and I joined the small crowd that the song switched to a slow melody. People began strolling off the dance floor while others pulled their dates into their arms. Only then did I realize I'd abandoned Logan and he sat at our table alone with our drinks.

On my way back to him, I heard someone call my name. I automatically turned to the voice, and my breath involuntarily caught in my throat. *Aaron.*

"May I have this dance?" he asked.

Sure, was my initial reaction, but I didn't get the word out before I caught myself. "I—uh. I'm here with someone."

A confident smirk crossed Aaron's face. "So? It's just a dance. It's not like I'm asking you for a kiss." I noticed his eyebrows wiggle subtly at the word "kiss."

My mood shifted quickly. I had the urge to point out that he never asked for a kiss the first time, but I forced myself to remain calm. "I really don't think I should dance with you."

"Is everything all right?" a tenor voice asked from beside me.

I jumped. I hadn't heard Logan approach. "It's fine," I answered, taking Logan's hand in my own. I shot Aaron a glare while stepping closer to Logan to show him where my true alliance lied.

Aaron held his hands up in surrender. "Sorry. I just thought one dance wouldn't hurt. It's not like I'm asking for another kiss."

My eyes widened at Aaron. How could he?

"Logan, let's dance." I tugged at his hand, but he remained grounded.

"What do you mean by that?" he directed at Aaron like he hadn't even heard me.

Aaron's eyebrows shot up, and a smirk formed across his face.

"Logan," I insisted, pulling at him harder now. "Let's just go."

His feet remained planted, and he narrowed his eyes at Aaron. It was like he couldn't even feel me pulling at him.

Aaron crossed his arms in amusement. "So, she didn't tell you?"

"Aaron," I snapped. "Just stop it." My words didn't seem to matter to him. His challenging gaze remained locked on Logan.

"Tell me what?" Logan finally glanced at me.

Water rose to my eyes. I couldn't. I just couldn't tell him the truth. "Aaron's just being dumb. Can we please go now?"

Logan started to follow me, but Aaron spoke again to stop us both. "I kissed her earlier this week."

We both stopped in our tracks and glared back at him, though for different reasons. Before either of us could respond, Aaron added what he knew would make Logan snap.

"And she kissed me back."

I didn't even have time to process the next split second before it was over. Logan lunged, and suddenly, a whish of cold air rushed in to fill the space where his hand had just been connected to mine. I heard the thud as his fist connected with Aaron's jaw, but I could barely believe my own ears. Though it was a well-deserved swing, all Aaron did was stumble back a step. When he absorbed the situation a moment later, he let his hand drop from his jaw where he'd reflexively placed it. Then he flung himself back toward Logan. In less than a second, they were on the ground.

"Stop it!" I shouted at them.

I glanced up nervously to notice that even though the

music still pulsed throughout the gym, people were beginning to stop and stare. A few students at tables across the room rose to get a good look. Two male chaperones—a teacher named Mr. Nelson and someone's parent I didn't recognize—were already on their way over to break up the fight.

"Stop!" I shouted again, hoping they'd listen before the chaperones intervened.

They each threw another punch like they never heard me. Questions raced through mind at lightning speed. *What can I say to make them stop? How do I get them to listen to me? Which one should I try to rescue?*

"Stop!" I shouted again because it's all I could think of to do. Any normal girl would wait another two seconds for the chaperones to reach us and pull them off each other, but I was determined to put an end to this fist fight as soon as possible. Before consciously deciding to, I fell to my knees and wedged my arms between their chests. I used all my strength to push against them and pry their bodies apart, but they both continued throwing punches like I wasn't there. I attempted to go in deeper and put myself between them so they'd stop. Not a great idea.

An elbow connected with my face, and then everything went black.

CHAPTER 18

AARON

I wasn't surprised when I awoke Saturday morning and saw that my bedroom was flooded with light. Aaron was right; I needed my sleep. I glanced over at the clock to see that it was already ten a.m. I groaned as I rolled out of bed and headed to the shower.

After blow drying my hair and slipping into something comfortable, I texted Alaina to confirm our plans for the day. I'd missed dress shopping with my friends, and I didn't want to miss out on the prep with our hair and makeup, too. Even though Aaron would be picking me up at my house later, I planned to get ready with my friends at Alaina's house.

I greeted her parents when I arrived and then headed down the hall to her bedroom. I knocked lightly on the door before pushing it open. Six eyes stared back at me.

"Come on in," Alaina greeted. She sat on the bed behind Emily and helped twist her hair into some sort of knot. Holly sat next to Alaina's mirror and attempted to tame her natural dark curls.

"Hey, chica," Emily said to me. "Whatcha got there?"

I held up the bag I'd brought. "This? Just my dress, shoes, and some hair pieces I thought some of you might want to try out. Didn't you say you were wearing a green dress, Alaina? I found this cute green bow in Kayla's room." I held it out to her.

"Thanks, but I already have a green headband." Her eyes drifted to her desk where the headband sat.

I set my bag on the floor. "Oh, cool. I like the color."

"Thanks," Alaina said with a smile.

I inhaled a deep breath. I'd worried at first that she'd still be harboring some ill feelings toward me for missing her art night, but she seemed to be over it—or at least pretending to be for my sake. At the very least, she welcomed me into her room, and that helped ease my anxiety.

"Want to see my dress?" Emily cut in. Before I could answer, she pulled away from Alaina and leaned over the side of the bed to reach the dress she'd laid out on the floor.

"Hey!" Alaina had to practically dive to keep ahold of the knot she was twisting in Emily's golden hair.

Emily looked back at her. "Whoops." She sprang back up and held the white dress out in front of her.

I sank to the ground and crossed my legs. "Cute. What's your dress like, Holly?"

She didn't look up from the mirror. "It's hanging on the back of Alaina's door."

I gazed over at the door and noticed it for the first time. It was a gorgeous royal blue cocktail dress with a halter top.

"Show us yours," Emily insisted with enthusiasm.

I pulled it out of the bag and held it up.

Emily's eyebrows came together. "That looks familiar. Have you worn it before?"

"It's Amy's dress, so you probably saw it on her or in pictures." I folded the dress back up and placed it in my bag.

"Right," Emily said. "I think I do remember her wearing that, was it two years ago?"

I shrugged.

"Did you hear the good news?" Holly asked, shooting a glance at Alaina.

A blush rose to Alaina's cheeks.

I glanced between the two of them. "No, I didn't. What's up?"

Alaina shrugged like it didn't matter. "I got second place in that art show. It's not a big deal, really. The awards are just for fun."

Alaina made it out to sound like it didn't mean anything to her, but I could tell it did. It sent that guilty sensation back into my gut for missing it. I hadn't even gone later in the week to check out the art like I said I would. I kind of hated myself for that.

"Hey, do you want me to do your hair?" Emily asked me, breaking the awkward silence that had followed Alaina's announcement.

"Don't let her!" Holly cried in jest.

I relaxed and laughed back. "It can't be that bad. What were your ideas, Emily?"

She pointed to her bag on the floor. "I brought a curling iron. Maybe I can curl your hair."

"Oh, uh." I reached up to run my fingers through my hair. "I can curl my own hair."

"Oh, come on," Emily encouraged. "Alaina's doing my hair. I want to do someone's hair."

I sighed and shifted until my back rested against the bed

below her. Then I twisted to look up at her. "Fine. Do your worst."

"My worst?" Her jaw dropped open in exaggerated offense. "Girl, I'm a miracle worker. Watch me work my magic."

Alaina pulled at Emily's hair. "Does any of your magic involve sitting still?"

Emily didn't waste any time reaching over to grab one of Alaina's decorative pillows to lightly toss it at her face.

I spent the next couple of hours laughing with my friends and letting Emily doll me up. Eventually, it came time for the festivities to begin.

"Aaron's picking me up at home," I reminded my friends.

Alaina glanced out her bedroom window. "Did you ride your bike here?"

"Um, yeah," I answered as I gathered the rest of my belongings.

"You're going to ride back in your dress?"

She had a point, but I just said, "It'll be fine."

Emily frowned. "But what about your hair?"

Before I could answer, Holly piped up. "Why don't you and Aaron just come with us tonight?"

I gazed down at my shoes and newly painted toenails. "He wanted to take me to dinner, for it to be just us." When I lifted my eyes, all three of them were starting at me intensely. "But I'll see you guys at the dance."

Alaina sighed. "At least let me drive you home real quick. We'll take my parents' van and put your bike in the back."

A half-smile formed across my face. I hated ditching my friends again—that's what it felt like even though we'd discussed the plan—but at least Alaina was being nice about it. "Thank you."

She turned back to Holly and Emily. "I'll be back in a

couple of minutes, girls. Unless either of you wants to come along?"

Emily shrugged. "Nah. It's a short drive. We'll stay in case the guys show up a little early."

"Okay," Alaina said, grabbing her purse from the floor and digging inside it for her keys.

The drive back to my house wasn't long, but it seemed longer than usual in the silence. It was the first time Alaina and I had been alone since the night I'd missed her art show and found her waiting at my house to chew me out for it. By the time she turned onto my street, neither of us had said anything. Usually we never ran out of things to talk about, so the silence left me wondering if she had truly forgiven me or if she'd just been playing along in front of our friends. Only, if she was still mad at me, why had she offered to drive me home?

My hand rested against the door handle when she stopped the van in my driveway, but I couldn't bring myself to exit without saying something. "Alaina," I started.

She looked up from the cuticles she was picking at. I could tell she was trying not to mess up the nail polish Emily had painted on her earlier. "Yeah?"

I took a deep breath and decided it didn't matter how uncomfortable I made things. I had to spit the words out. "Are you still mad at me?"

"What?" She laughed like the idea was ridiculous, but I could tell the laugh was forced.

I dropped my hand from the door, realizing this might take longer than I'd anticipated. "You are, aren't you? I don't know how I can show you that I'm sorry for missing your art night. Do you want me to admit I was a total jerk? Because I was."

She gave a half-hearted smile without looking at me. "That's a good start." Her words stung a little, but I deserved them.

"I know it meant a lot to you."

Finally, she lifted her gaze and spoke slowly. "You don't even realize what I'm mad about, do you?"

Didn't I? My whole body tensed. "Well, I missed your art night, and that meant something to you."

She nodded. "Yeah, but the art night isn't what the big deal was."

I furrowed my brow. "I don't understand."

"It's *you*, Maddie," she emphasized. "I've been mad because you've stopped being *you*. I thought that if I acted like things were okay, then maybe they would be, but I don't know how much longer I can keep pretending. It seems like you're still trying to be someone you're not." She sighed and dropped her gaze again. "I wish you'd hang out with us more like you used to."

Tears rose to my eyes. "I already made plans with Aaron tonight."

"I know." She forced a smile again. "Just don't cut me out completely, okay?"

"Alaina." My stern voice got her to look up at me again. A line of tears had settled along her lower lid. I could tell she was trying to hold it back so it wouldn't mess up her makeup. "I will *never* stop being your best friend. Next week, I'm back to sitting by you at lunch, back to our after school hangouts, okay?"

Her lips twitched like she was fighting a genuine smile.

"I mean, you'll still have to share me, just like I share you with Jordan," I told her.

"I know." Her voice cracked as she blinked away the water

in her eyes. "I just don't want to lose you. You're my best friend."

"Hey," I said softly. I leaned across the space between our seats to pull her into a hug. "I promise you'll never lose me."

She sniffled. "Thanks, Maddie." She pulled away and dabbed her fingers at her eyes, careful not to mess up her makeup. "Now, go have fun. I'll see you at the dance."

I blinked and sniffled just like she had. "You, too. I'll see you soon."

"Bye." She waved as I stepped out of the van and headed to the back to get my bike.

It was only a few minutes after I placed my bike in the garage that Aaron showed up on my doorstep. "There's my gorgeous angel," he greeted with a kiss.

"Come in, Aaron!" my mother called from behind me. I turned to see she had her camera ready for a photo shoot.

My hands reflexively shot up in front of my face. "No, Mom!"

"Oh, come on," my father encouraged as he entered the room. "You need to cherish the memories."

I dropped my hand. "I'll remember the night without the pictures."

"Nothing's wrong with taking a few pictures," Aaron encouraged. His hand settled on my waist, and he pulled me into him.

I had the sudden urge to push him away, but I didn't. Instead, I stared into the camera and put on the most genuine-looking smile I could muster. *Would my parents be doing this if I had any other boyfriend? Or are they just acting like this because they like Aaron?* Somehow, I knew their excitement stemmed from their adoration of Aaron and the entire Harding family.

"There." My mom shut off her camera. "See? That wasn't so bad."

I kissed them both goodbye and then took Aaron's hand as we headed out the door.

My father waved. "You two have fun! Don't stay out all night."

Before we even made it out of the driveway, Aaron asked, "So, are you having fun yet?"

"The night hasn't even started." I didn't like the way my voice came out sounding, so I tried again in a softer tone. "But you're here, so I have high hopes for the rest of the night."

Aaron beamed at me.

"Where are we going for dinner?" I asked.

His gaze drifted over to me without turning his head. "You'll see."

"Ugh," I complained. "I hate surprises."

The corners of his lips turned down. A wave of guilt hit me like I'd said something wrong. He didn't take his eyes off the road, but he shifted his hands on the steering wheel.

"You really don't like surprises, do you?" he asked.

I knotted my hands in my lap. "I really don't."

Aaron sighed, but his expression told me I wasn't being as annoying as I felt I was. He almost looked *amused*.

I reflexively tucked my hair behind my ear. "What?"

He shrugged. "I didn't say anything."

"But you're thinking something you're not saying."

The grin he'd been holding back broke across his face. "I think it's cute."

"Cute?" I guess I should have taken it as a compliment, right?

"Well, you have a *thing*, you know?"

I didn't answer because I wasn't sure I *did* know. My hair was cute. My dress was cute. My attitude? Not so much.

"We're almost there. Think you can hold out?"

"I guess so," I answered dully. I didn't know what else to do with myself, so I rested an elbow on my door and stared out the window. Though I was looking outside, I wasn't really paying attention to where we were headed.

"Hey," Aaron said softly, reaching over to touch my left hand. "What's wrong?"

I didn't realize I had been chewing on my lip until I opened my mouth to speak. "Nothing's wrong." I threw in a good shoulder shrug.

"You just seem kind of… I don't know… disengaged. Uninterested. Is it the surprise thing? I'll tell you where we're going. Actually, we're almost there already."

Aaron pulled into a parking space alongside the street. When I finally took in my surroundings, I realized we were in the older part of town. I scanned the shops in front of us and saw we were parked close to the pizza place we'd visited a few weeks ago.

I shot Aaron a smile to help lighten the mood. "Pizza sounds perfect. Thank you."

"See? Surprises aren't that bad. Stay here for a second." He hopped out of the car and rounded the front side to open my door as if to prove his point.

This time, my smile was genuine. "You're such a gentleman." I intended the statement to come out lighthearted and silly, but I spoke so much truth that it didn't sound at all like I was teasing him.

He shrugged as he shut the door behind me. "I try."

I giggled and took his hand as we walked to the pizzeria. There weren't a lot of people there, just a group of students in their homecoming dress near the window and a family of four in the booth next to them. Aaron led me to the back table where we sat the first time we ate here.

"Half Hawaiian and half pepperoni?" Aaron asked.

I pressed my lips together in thought. "Surprise me?"

"I thought you didn't like surprises."

My eyes dropped to the napkin I'd already begun twisting around in my hands. "Well, they aren't all that bad."

Laughter erupted from Aaron's lungs.

My heart skipped a beat in surprise. "What's so funny?"

"I—I don't know," he said between giggles. He quieted by the time he spoke again. "You're just amusing, is all. Okay. A surprise it is."

Not long afterward, I was chewing on stuffed crust pepperoni and sausage pizza while admiring the crane I'd made from my napkin after following Aaron's tutorial. His watchful gaze made my cheeks flame, but I tried to pretend like it was nothing. Hopefully Emily slathered on enough makeup that it didn't show.

Just as I was about to break the silence with some stupid description of how good the pizza tasted, something warm touched my leg. My heart skipped another beat, this time for good reasons. Aaron's ankle slithered its way up my leg. By the time his foot reached my knee, more nerves had overtaken my body than I could handle.

I playfully shoved his foot back to the floor. "Behave yourself."

"Hey," he teased, "I can't always be a gentleman. It's a lot of hard work, you know."

I couldn't contain my laughter, but of course, it had to be just as I bit into my pizza, so a string of cheese ran between my mouth and my food. By the time I managed to swallow, pizza grease covered my chin. Aaron reached across the table to hand me a new napkin.

"Thanks." I wiped at my chin, hoping my makeup wasn't too messed up. When I glanced back up at Aaron, I stopped everything. Laughing. Moving. Breathing. I looked into his eyes and saw all the good times we shared together. *This is where I'm meant to be,* I thought. A moment later, I snapped out of my trance. "Thanks for bringing me tonight. But I'm afraid that if I eat more pizza, I might explode. That wouldn't be good for my dress."

"No, we certainly wouldn't want any *clothing* exploding tonight." He bit his lip lightly and looked across the table at me under his dark lashes.

Did he mean what I think he meant?

"Well," he said after composing himself, "I guess we can split the rest and each take some home. Are you ready for the dance?"

"Yes!" I answered with more enthusiasm than I'd felt all week. It was like Aaron had the magic power to make me feel all better again. *And that's why I love him so much.*

When we stepped into the high school gymnasium, I spotted my friends immediately. I took a step in their direction the same time Aaron headed toward his friends. He didn't seem to notice the split second where the distance between us grew. I quickly realized my mistake and followed him, my hand entwined with his. I didn't like this, though. Hadn't I just promised Alaina I'd hang out with her more? Why did Aaron's friends get priority over mine?

"Oh my gosh!" Dani raved as soon as Aaron and I were within earshot. "Your dress is *so* pretty." She wore a deep red dress with see-through lace sleeves.

"Yours, too," I told her.

"Here, I saved you a seat." Dani gestured to the chair beside her, and I sat.

Aaron took the empty seat next to me. "Anything interesting happen yet?" he asked the group.

They all shrugged.

"They've only played one slow song since we got here," Dani complained.

"What's wrong with fast songs?" Aaron gestured to the small crowd jumping up and down on the dance floor. I noticed Jordan in the middle of the mix busting his moves.

Dani's mouth hung open for a second before speaking. "I'll make a fool out of myself!"

Her boyfriend, Brandon, sat back in his chair with his arms crossed over his chest. He scowled toward the dance floor. It's like he thought he was too good to be caught dancing.

Aaron laughed at Dani. "But you're a cheerleader. Aren't you supposed to dance?"

"That's different," Dani defended. "We choreograph our dances."

Aaron raised his brows as if to say, *You got me there.* "Well, I don't know about you, but this is a *dance,* and I came here to dance." He stood and held his hand out to me. "Would you like to join me?"

I glanced back at the crowd. I wasn't exactly an avid dancer, but I longed to hang out with my friends. A couple of them were on the dance floor, and it might be my only chance tonight to enjoy it with them. *Why didn't I just go with them?* I caught myself thinking. *What did I miss out on by going with Aaron instead?* I forced my eyes back toward Aaron because I knew he was waiting for an answer. "Sure."

Once we stepped onto the dance floor, I found my way

over to Holly and Emily and mimicked their motions. Mostly, it was jumping up and down, but I still felt silly. Aaron stayed close.

"Hey, Maddie," they both greeted together over the sound of the music.

I smiled back. "Are you guys having fun?"

"What?" Holly asked, moving in closer to hear me.

"I said, are you having fun?"

"Yeah!"

I didn't try talking again because it was hard to hear anyone with the speakers blasting next to us. So instead, I just jumped up and down and watched Jordan take the spotlight. A few students nearby were grinding against each other, but it wasn't long before a chaperone came up to scold them. The two separated, and the girl ran off toward the bathroom in anger.

When the song shifted, Aaron pulled me into his arms and swayed back and forth with me. We didn't say a thing. That gave me time for my eyes to wander. I noticed Alaina and Jordan nearby in an embrace. Holly and Blake danced together next to them, and Emily and her date swayed on the other end of the dance floor. Someone was missing. I scanned the tables and chairs across the room for any sign of Logan. *Did he even come?* Disappointment that I couldn't quite explain washed over me when I realized that was a very real possibility. Still, I continued my search.

By the last chorus of the song, I had determined he wasn't there. A moment later, I spotted his wispy blond hair in the doorway. He entered the gym and headed over to the same table I saw my friends sitting at earlier. *He must have just been in the bathroom,* I figured.

The song ended, and Aaron and I parted.

"I'm going to get a drink," he told me.

"Okay."

He headed off, and I crossed the dance floor in the opposite direction. Alaina was on her way back to her table after the slow song, but I caught her before she made it.

"Hey, Alaina."

She turned to me. "Yeah?" Her voice was upbeat and happy.

"How's Logan doing?"

She glanced at him quickly. He didn't pay us any attention. "Oh, uh, I think he's fine, but he doesn't have a date. I feel kind of bad for him."

I frowned. "Yeah, I kind of do, too."

"Well, I know Emily said there was this girl in choir who would have gone with him if he asked her. I think she was talking about Jennifer." Alaina crossed her arms over her chest. "It's kind of by choice that he didn't come with a date."

At least he had the choice, but what did that mean? That he didn't want to date anyone unless it was me? Or did it have nothing to do with me at all? Maybe it was just my narcissism, but something told me that it had *everything* to do with me.

Logan's lyrics darted into my head in that moment. *We could have been something great.*

Maybe, I thought, *but now we'll never know.* I didn't realize how long I stared in his direction until Alaina's voice broke my trance.

"Do you want to go over there and talk to him?" she asked.

"What?" I shook my head. "No. I think that would just be awkward for both of us."

"You could come over and sit by me. I could use the company."

"Don't you want to dance?" I glanced back at the group on

the floor and saw that Aaron had returned from getting his drink. He moved almost as confidently as Jordan.

Alaina shrugged. "I'm not really a dancer, and it doesn't help when your boyfriend is a million times better than you. Besides, then Logan would be all alone at our table."

I glanced between her and Logan and then back at Aaron. "I guess I'll join you." I was interested in seeing how Logan was doing, and Aaron seemed to be having enough fun that he wouldn't notice my absence. Logan looked up at us as we approached the table, but he didn't say anything. In fact, none of us said anything throughout the next several songs. I had a feeling my presence was the source of the awkward energy surrounding our table.

After several songs, Aaron surprised me by making his way to my friends' table where I sat. "There you are!" He placed a light kiss on my forehead. "You ran off on me. Do you want a drink or anything?"

I shook my head. "No, I'm fine."

"Anyone else?" he asked, addressing Logan and Alaina.

I didn't miss the scowl Logan shot back at him. They both declined his offer.

"Okay," Aaron said and then directed his attention back to me. "I'll be back in a bit. You should get out on the dance floor for the next song. It's a lot of fun."

I managed to muster a shy smile. "Okay."

Aaron hurried out of the doors of the gymnasium, presumably to stop at the bathroom. Just as he exited the doors, the melody shifted, and a slow song came on. Alaina stood to join Jordan on the dance floor, leaving Logan and me in awkward silence.

"I thought you were going to dance the next song," Logan

pointed out. His attempt at conversation caught me slightly off guard. I'd figured he was still upset at me.

"Well, yeah, but Aaron isn't back yet," I said softly while gazing down at my hands knotted in my lap.

"You don't need Aaron to dance," he pointed out.

"Well, how else would I dance to a slow song?" Heat rushed to my cheeks when I lifted my eyes to look at him.

He raised his eyebrows. "You could dance with me."

My breath caught in my throat. *That* was the surprise of the night. "I could, but…"

"Just one song?" he pleaded. "You owe it to me."

I furrowed my brow. "How do you figure that?"

Logan let out a laugh, and it softened my mood. "I don't know. I just thought that might get you out on the dance floor with me." His smile was infectious.

"Okay," I breathed. After all, Aaron did say I should get out on the dance floor for the next song, and seeing as he wasn't there at the moment, I'd take the one partner I could find. "But just as friends."

"Just as friends," Logan confirmed.

I held his left hand in my right and settled my other hand on his shoulder, keeping a generous amount of distance between our bodies. I didn't think *friends* danced with their bodies slammed against each other the way Aaron and I had been dancing earlier. Logan didn't seem to mind the distance. The first few moments of silence between us felt more awkward than the last several minutes seated at his table combined. It was probably because I was forced to look at him.

"So," I started in an attempt to minimize the awkwardness. "Do anything fun lately?"

"You mean, besides make a complete and utter fool out of myself? No."

I tilted my head in confusion until I realized what he was referring to. "Complete and utter fool? You mean singing that song to me? It wasn't that bad."

Logan's gaze dropped to his feet. "Well, it sure felt like it."

"Excuse me," another voice cut in.

My gaze darted over to Aaron, who stood just feet away from me. I hadn't even heard him approach. I dropped my hand from Logan's shoulder, but his grip tightened on my right hand.

"Oh," I said. "We were just—" I glanced between both of them.

"Dancing," Logan finished for me. He continued to lead me around in a circle even though Aaron stood right there, ready to lay his rightful claim on me.

"As *friends*," I clarified, shooting a glance at Logan.

"Perhaps I can cut in now," Aaron suggested lightly, but the look on his face didn't match his tone.

I was about to pull away from Logan and join Aaron when Logan tightened his hold around my waist.

"She promised me one song. That's it," Logan said without ceasing our swaying.

Aaron's expression grew more distressed. "Well, I'm here now, and I'm her boyfriend. So I'll take over."

At this point, it didn't sound like I had a say in it. This was no longer about who got to dance with me. They fought over me like they thought whoever finished the song with me would end up with me forever.

"If you guys don't stop, I'm not dancing with anyone." My voice came out strong and confident. I had no idea how I managed that considering I felt more nervous than anything.

Logan's grip on my hand tightened so much that the ends of my fingers began turning red. Aaron was practically blowing smoke from his nostrils now.

"You don't have the right to dance with her." Aaron's typical calm voice held an edge of anger that I'd never heard before.

"It was her choice," Logan bit back.

I was about to set them straight again and tell them that I was done dancing, that I didn't want to dance with either of them, but before I could, Aaron's arms dove between Logan and me in an attempt to force us apart.

"Just let her go!" Aaron shouted.

Logan did let me go but only so he could retaliate. His fist came out to connect with Aaron's shoulder.

Okay. I lied earlier. *This* was definitely the surprise of the night.

Aaron shot back with a punch to Logan's jaw.

"Stop it!" I called to them both, but they continued like they didn't hear me. Any rational girl would have waited for a chaperone to rush over and break up their fight. They were probably already on their way, but I didn't take the time to look up and process my surroundings. No doubt people were already starting to stare. But I was already in the middle of this, and I dove in further by throwing my body between them. "Stop it!" I shouted again.

And that's when a fist connected with my face. Somehow, I knew I was going down, but I couldn't control it. The gymnasium faded to black, and I hit the floor.

That's when I remembered.

Everything.

CHAPTER 19

I opened my eyes to twinkling lights above me. What had happened? Oh, right. Some idiot had knocked me out. Twice.

I quickly became aware that I was lying on my back on the gymnasium floor, staring up at the lights the dance committee had hung from the ceiling. Both Logan's and Aaron's faces came into view. I glanced between them both.

My eyes first fell on Aaron. Aaron, the guy who had taken me on an adventure through the mall, who had built a sheet fort with me in his living room, who had convinced me to join cheerleading and helped me make friends I never would have thought I'd like.

My gaze flickered to Logan's. Logan, the guy who had shared his beautiful lyrics with me, who had taken me to see *Beauty and the Beast*, who had surprised me with a romantic picnic at a beautiful waterfall.

I stared back at Aaron. He was also the guy who told me I'd made the wrong choice and kissed me uninvitingly.

I shifted my attention back to Logan. He was the guy who told me he still had feelings for me through a song.

All of these thoughts flickered through my head before anyone even had a chance to speak. How was it that I remembered two different realities, one as equal as the other? The scariest part? I remembered them both so vividly that I had no idea which one I was living in at the moment.

"Are you okay?" Aaron and Logan both asked at the same time.

I didn't answer right away. How did this happen? Did the punch to my face cause brain damage? Had I dreamt the other reality while I was out cold? It didn't matter what theories I came up with to make rational sense out of the situation. I knew the truth. Chloe's "splitting your heart in two" thing had worked. The lady was the real deal. But hadn't she warned me about something? *I must warn you that if you change your mind about the boy you choose, you risk losing them both,* she had said.

Now I knew what she meant. The moment I started questioning my decision—when Aaron kissed me and when Logan sang me his "pieces of dreams" song—my two worlds began to collide. And now? Now I remembered how amazing and equally frustrating it was to be with and without each of them. My heart once again ached for them both, and it sent me straight back to square one at lightning speed. I had no idea which one I was supposed to be with.

The realization hit me only a split second after they both asked if I was okay. Though I was physically fine—apart from a pounding headache—I wasn't okay. I couldn't even remember if I'd been hit with an elbow or a fist.

"We're so sorry," Logan said as he and Aaron reached down to grab my arms and pull me to a seated position.

Aaron cupped my face in his hands and stared into my

eyes, probably looking for signs of a concussion. I swatted his hands away. This was too much to deal with. Was I supposed to love him, or was I supposed to be upset that he kissed me without an invitation?

When I glanced to Logan, the same conflicted emotions hit me. Should I be throwing myself into his arms or cursing him for… for what? Had he really done anything wrong? He sang me a song. He asked me to dance. Was that so bad? Yet he'd still done the same as Aaron had. He tried to get me to change my mind.

One more flicker of my gaze between the two of them, and I knew. Though I remembered thinking to myself that I was *supposed* to be with each of them when I was with them, I knew there was only one person I could truly count on when it came to love. I knew who I had to choose. And I knew I needed Chloe to help set this madness straight.

They both stared at me expectantly, and my mind began to clear. I noticed for the first time that a group had formed around us and that the music had stopped. Mr. Nelson knelt beside Logan and tried to get everyone else to back away and give me space.

"I—" I managed to croak out, just barely. I cleared my throat and tried again. This time, my voice came out strong and confident. "I have to go."

And then I sprang to my feet and pushed through the crowd before anyone could grab ahold of me and slow me down. I burst through the gym doors and out into the chilly darkness. I didn't slow my feet as I raced the few blocks back home. Only silence followed. I expected at least *someone* to come after me, but I was thankful they didn't. I wouldn't have been able to outrun them in my heels. Either way, I entered my house and rushed up to my bedroom alone.

My father poked his head out of his office as I pounded up the stairs. "Everything all right, Maddie?"

"I'm fine, Dad," I called back down the stairs. It wasn't true. The pounding in my head was only growing more intense, but I couldn't deal with any questions from him or my mom right now. In my bedroom, I stripped off my jewelry and tossed it into my jewelry box. I wasn't entirely sure which piece I'd just taken off, but perhaps in a way, I'd managed both. However it happened, the bracelet and necklace were both there.

I hurried down the stairs as quickly as I had raced up them. At the bottom, I placed a kiss on my father's cheek. "I'm fine, Daddy. I just had to get something. I'll see you later."

He stared after me speechlessly as I raced to the garage and grabbed my bike. I held the jewelry box in one hand and steered my bike with the other. The whole time, I chanted in my head *Please be there, Chloe. Please be there, Chloe.* Yeah, it was late, but the girl managed to *split* my heart. She must have had some sort of magic that told her I was on my way.

The bike ride to Chloe's shop seemed twice as long as I thought it'd be, but eventually, I made it. I dropped my bike onto the sidewalk and tried the door. Of course, it was locked. I desperately banged on it and called out to Chloe.

"Okay, I'm here! I get it now. I know who I have to choose. Chloe?" I peered into the shop window the best I could, but inside was pitch black. The street lamp near me only illuminated the first few feet of the shop. "Chloe?" I called again.

Nothing. I sighed and turned from the door. My gaze shifted up and down the street like I might find an answer there, but it was no use. Now that I wasn't moving, I realized how cold it was. I crossed my arms over my chest for warmth, the jewelry box still in my hand. Just as I'd resolved to giving up, a voice spoke my name from behind me. A surge of hope coursed through me as I turned back toward the shop door. Chloe's smiling face stared back at me.

"Please, come in." She opened the door wider, and I slipped inside.

"You knew I'd be back," I stated. I planted my feet near the dream catchers and stared into her face.

She didn't look the least bit confused. "It was a possibility."

"A possibility?"

Chloe kindly gestured for me to follow her, and she led me past the beaded curtain into the pink room I'd been in the first time I visited. She explained before sitting down. "Maddie, I can't see a definite future. I can only see *possibilities*. We all have free will. I wasn't sure if you'd come back or not because it was your *choice*. You see?"

I sank into the chair across from her. As soon as I sat, exhaustion hit. "I'm not sure. You said you had a feeling I'd be back, didn't you?"

She spoke in the same slow, melodic voice I'd heard before. "I did have a feeling. I also had a feeling you wouldn't return."

"Okay." I spoke the word slowly. I wasn't entirely sure I understood, but there were more pressing matters to get to. "So, you know who I'm going to choose now?"

Chloe shook her head. Her strawberry blond curls swayed across her shoulders. "There are many possible outcomes. The decision is yours."

I nodded. I was beginning to understand. "But you can reverse it, right?" *Please, tell me you can reverse it. I can't live in two realities forever.*

Chloe gave me another friendly smile. "I can't."

My heart immediately dropped in my chest. *Then why are you smiling at me?* I wanted to say.

"But you can," she stated.

At least there was hope, but what did that mean? I wasn't gifted in the paranormal like she was. I hadn't spent years traveling the world studying it. I didn't have the slightest clue on how to reverse this whole thing, to get back to a single reality. Chloe must have noticed the worry on my face because she offered to clarify.

"You have to make your decision, and then everything will go back to the way it's supposed to be."

I let out the breath I didn't realize I was holding. That was it? It was that simple? I drew in another long breath. Okay. I was ready. Chloe didn't say anything as I pulled open the jewelry box.

I stared down into the box, knowing this was the easiest decision I'd ever made. This was the obvious decision all along, the one I should have made weeks ago. The angel wing pendant sat on one side, the purple bracelet on the other. In between them, my rose ring. I noticed immediately how symbolic it seemed, how the jewelry box was split into two sections and the one piece of jewelry I had that represented *me* sat in the middle. I reached into the box and then held the rose ring up so Chloe could see it.

"Me. I choose me."

CHAPTER 20

When I lifted my gaze from the ring on my finger, Chloe held her fists out in my direction. Confusion overtook me.

"So, which boy will it be?" she asked. "Logan, or Aaron?"

I glanced around quickly. Where had my jewelry box gone? Another look down at my hand told me I still wore the rose ring, but then I noticed something else. Instead of the homecoming dress I was in just moments before, I wore jeans. Realization washed over me, and I gently pushed Chloe's hands away. "Neither."

A smile slowly crept across her face. "So, will you be needing these back?" She opened her hands to reveal the two pieces of jewelry in them.

"No," I almost answered, but I paused mid-breath. I wouldn't be needing them, but the least I could do was give them back to the owners. "Actually, yeah. I'll take them."

After slipping them in my pocket, I handed all the cash I had across the table. "Thank you for your help."

"Anytime," she responded with a smile.

I stood and took the few steps toward the beaded curtain. Before I crossed through it, I inhaled a deep breath. I closed my eyes and pushed through the waterfall of beads. When I opened them, the first thing I noticed was the light flooding the room. I'd walked in here at dark and came out in mid-day. And then I spotted Alaina, just as I expected to find her.

"How'd it go?" she asked.

I smiled. "I made a decision. Come on, I'll tell you about it in the car." Before I made it out the door, I heard the beads in the doorway again. I turned back to Chloe, who wore a knowing smile on her face. "Thank you," I told her one last time before following Alaina out the door.

"So," Alaina dragged out the word as she buckled herself in the driver's seat. "Who'd you choose?"

I let the silence hang there for a moment to draw out the suspense. I also wasn't sure if she would understand my decision. How could I tell her I hadn't chosen either of them?

"Come on," she encouraged. "Didn't the psychic lady help you?"

"She did, but the thing is, I didn't choose Logan or Aaron."

"What?" Alaina took her foot off the gas for a second and stared at me in surprise. "I thought you said she helped you."

I nodded. "She did. And I decided that I don't need either of them. I chose me." I pointed to my own chest proudly.

"Wow," Alaina said in admiration. "I didn't even think of that as an option. And you know what?" Her gaze flickered to mine then back on the road. "I think it's the best decision you've ever made. Hey, is that Chinese place on this block or the next one?"

Oh, yeah! I completely forgot about going out for Chinese. Yum! "It's past that stop light. Oh, and Alaina?"

"Yeah?"

"I'd like to submit a drawing for the art night. What do you think? Will you help me choose one?"

She beamed back at me. "I'd love to help!"

Even though I didn't choose Logan or Aaron, I decided I couldn't just leave them hanging. The next morning, I texted them both at breakfast asking them to meet me at the café for lunch. Logan texted back right away agreeing to the meeting, and Aaron's text came shortly afterward.

In my room, I browsed through my shirt drawer and wondered what to wear. At the bottom of my drawer, I found a purple dolman style t-shirt that I hadn't worn in months because both Aaron and Logan said they hated the style. I liked it, so I slipped it on. At the mirror, I pulled half of my hair up and secured it with bobby pins while the other half hung loose around my shoulders. *This is me*, I thought as I stared back at myself. I didn't have to impress anyone, and for the first time in a long time, I felt truly comfortable with myself.

Before leaving, I double checked that I had their jewelry with me and that my ring was still on my finger. It was. Then I hopped on my bike and pedaled to the café. I expected to arrive first, but as soon as I entered, I spotted Logan and Aaron seated next to each other in a booth. They both noticed me, and they watched as I crossed the room and slid into the seat across from them.

Our waitress, Laura, showed up at our table as soon as I sat down. "Can I get you anything to drink?"

"No," I told her. "I'm good, thanks."

Aaron didn't waste a second as soon as she walked away, although I didn't expect him to. "So, Maddie, who is it going to be?"

Both of their faces had fallen like they already expected me to choose the other guy. I knew two hearts would break today, but I also knew that this was what had to be done. They would heal, and so would I.

"Well…" I reached into my pocket and placed each piece of jewelry in front of their respective owner.

Both Logan's and Aaron's faces lit up when they saw their piece of jewelry sitting in front of them. A split second later, they both noticed the other piece of jewelry on the table.

Logan frowned. "What does this mean?"

I placed my hand on the table in clear view, but I didn't bother explaining the significance of the ring on my finger. "I'm not choosing either of you."

"What?" they asked together. A look of shock hit them both.

"You can't just not make a decision," Aaron stated.

I blinked a few times. How couldn't he understand? "I did make a decision. And I chose neither of you. I chose me."

Logan's eyes narrowed in confusion. "You chose *you*?"

"Look." I leaned away from them until my back pressed up against the cushion behind me. "I need time to figure *me* out first before I throw someone else into the mix. I can either figure out who I am, or I'll end up changing to please someone else. I need time to learn more about myself. I hope we can all continue to be friends, though."

Though the announcement surprised them, they both relaxed their shoulders as if they accepted it.

Aaron was the first to compose himself. "Friends," he agreed.

Logan nodded his head along. "Of course we can still be friends."

"Thank you, guys," I told them as sincerely as I felt it.

They both reached out to take their own piece of jewelry back. It was like they were taking their romantic feelings back, too, a symbol that they really meant what they said about friendship.

EPILOGUE

"You're really going without a date?" Emily asked for about the hundredth time. She sat on the floor at the foot of Alaina's bed while Alaina helped twist her blond hair into a knot.

I had an odd sense of déjà vu, though I'd gotten used to that over the past several weeks. I reminded myself that the déjà vu would soon be over. On the bright side, my homework had been a breeze so far since I'd already done most of it twice. Though I'd experienced that feeling of having "been there before" often since school started, I still never quite knew what to expect. Going stag to the dance meant everything about tonight would be different—at least, I hoped.

"I really am," I answered. I stood in front of Alaina's full-length mirror attached to the back of her door and smoothed out my dress. I'd bought it at the mall when we went dress shopping last weekend. It was a deep purple fabric with spaghetti strap sleeves and rhinestones around the chest area. I absolutely loved it.

"You're brave," Holly said from across the room, where she twisted her own dark hair into an updo. "If I didn't have a date, I probably wouldn't be going."

I tore my gaze from the mirror and glanced down at the rose-shaped ring on my finger. "I have a date," I defended. "I'm going with myself."

Emily and Holly rolled their eyes in sync, but Holly was the one to speak. "I don't think that counts as a date."

"Okay," Emily said. She shifted slightly on the floor, which earned her a scolding from Alaina. "I just have to ask, Maddie. What exactly does this mean? Have you written off love forever? Are you *ever* going to have a boyfriend again?"

I laughed and leaned against the wall next to me. "Of course I'll have a boyfriend again! I just want to be a single for a while, figure *me* out first. I don't have to be with a guy just because he likes me. I don't *need* a boyfriend just to have one."

Emily took a deep breath. "But you're still keeping your options open, right?"

I nodded. "Right. I'm not going to completely write off love. If the right guy comes along… well, I wouldn't want to pass up that chance."

Alaina raised her eyebrows. "So you're saying neither Aaron nor Logan were the right guy?"

As much as I'd thought about this topic over the past several weeks, I'd mostly avoided talking about it with my friends. I didn't think they really understood where I was coming from, and how could they? They weren't there to experience it all.

"I think we're all better off being friends," I stated confidently.

Holly spoke while admiring her updo in the mirror. "I

really meant what I said, Maddie. You're brave." Her words came out sounding genuine this time.

"Thank you," I told her with a smile.

Emily glanced into the handheld mirror next to her while Alaina brushed away the last stray strands and locked her hair into place with a spritz of hairspray. "Are you ready for your beautifying session?" Emily asked me once she'd set the mirror back down. "You're already in your dress, so let's get to work on your hair."

"Beautifying session?" Alaina joked. "More like a torture session."

We all laughed together, but I gave in and let Emily do my hair. When she asked if I wanted it up or down, I told her half up and half down. With thick hair, I liked it best that way.

"Whatever you want," she agreed and then ran a brush through it.

Alaina hopped off the bed and grabbed her phone from her desk next to Holly. "You know what I forgot to do?" she asked. "I was so wrapped up in homecoming stuff that I forgot to check on the results of the art night." She typed something into her phone while she spoke. As soon as the web page loaded, she squealed. "Oh my gosh! Maddie, we both won!"

"What?" I asked in surprise, hopping up out of Emily's grasp to check out the screen.

"Yeah," Alaina said. "That picture of the flower garden got first, I got second, and you got third. Isn't that awesome!"

"Yeah!" I said back with an equal amount of enthusiasm. It's not like we won anything, just bragging rights, but I could hardly believe it. I mean, I felt bad that I kind of booted out whoever won third place while my heart was split—I never did catch who came in third—but I'd put a lot of work into my drawing of a rose, and I figured that in this version of reality, I deserved it.

It wasn't long after we'd all put the finishing touches on our hair and makeup that the doorbell rang, sending a rush of excitement through my body. We all hurried to the door and welcomed in our group of friends. Alaina's parents took pictures of us before we piled into Blake's mom's van. I was happy to see that Logan had brought a date along, a girl from choir named Jennifer. They sat in the back seat together next to Emily, whose date was meeting us at the café. I squeezed in next to Alaina and Jordan in the second row.

I hadn't talked much to Jennifer in the past, but as we all chatted throughout dinner, I came to like her more and more. She seemed nice. She talked about music when Emily brought it up, and she raved about Logan's guitar, Lucy.

I smiled at the mention of it. It sounded like Jennifer really enjoyed his songs. Maybe one day he'd write one for her. The thought warmed my heart, and I realized by the end of dinner that I could honestly say I was happy for Logan.

A slow song played through the speakers when we entered the gymnasium. My friends and I claimed a table at the edge of the dance floor, and most of them paired off to catch the end of the song. I stayed back, taking a seat at the table and angling my chair toward them to watch. Everyone, it seemed, was smiling, and I noticed a smile creep across my own face.

I caught a glimpse of Aaron on the dance floor. He spun in slow circles with a girl named Tess, one of Dani's friends from cheerleading. He threw his head back and laughed at something Tess said. I actually liked seeing him have fun without me.

Though I enjoyed seeing everyone so happy, my nerves

remained on edge. There was a slight sense of déjà vu here. The blue streamers and white table cloths brought back strong memories of the last time I'd been here. I half expected a fight to break out and leave me lying on the ground staring up at the twinkling Christmas lights.

When an upbeat tempo began playing, cutting through the slow, soft melody of the last song, I hopped up from my chair and joined my friends on the dance floor. Jordan busted his talented moves while Blake tried his hand at a few complicated moves, which didn't work out well for him. He didn't seem to notice.

My gaze drifted past Jordan to Logan and Aaron. My muscles tightened so much that I stopped dancing. The music seemed to fade, and my attention focused on the two guys. Their expressions both read aggression.

Are they going to fight again? I wondered. *Over what?*

Aaron moved, and for a moment, I was afraid he was going for Logan's face again. But then he backed away, almost in a hopping motion. Logan made his own move, and it was only a split second later that I realized they weren't fighting at all. They were having a *dance off*. Both of them eased their posture. Logan's eyes crinkled as he grinned, and I could faintly hear Aaron's laughter above the music. That's when the thumping bass came back into focus. Aaron held his hand out to Logan, and he shook it in that macho way guys do.

The tension in my shoulders eased. They were being *friendly* toward each other. It seemed so odd after everything I'd experienced. I didn't know if I'd ever get used to it—to them being friends—but it seemed like I'd made the right decision. When I turned them both down, they turned to each other and became friends because of it.

"Hey, Maddie!"

The sound of my name pulled me from my thoughts, and I sprang back to full attention, pulling my eyes off the laughing boys across the dance floor. I turned to the voice and found Dani bouncing on her feet to the beat.

"What are you just standing there for? Move your feet, girl!" She giggled, and I did as she instructed.

The one thing I missed about having my heart split was the friendship I'd built with Dani. Though I hadn't gone back into cheerleading, we'd still been assigned to the same group in English, and I was slowly building back up the friendship she never even knew existed. So far, we'd really connected.

"Having fun?" she shouted over the music.

I nodded.

"Still happy with your choice?" she asked.

I glanced across the dance floor to Aaron and Logan without consciously deciding to. They were engaged in another mini dance off and laughing hysterically at each other. A moment after I looked over there, I realized she couldn't be referring to them. She didn't know about that.

"Your dress," she clarified, still moving her body to the music. "You told me in English you weren't sure if you were going to get a new dress or borrow one from your sister."

"Right. I'm still happy with it. It was even on sale."

"Well, it's pretty!" she told me before turning to another group of people behind her.

In her absence, my gaze drifted once again across the dance floor. I found myself contemplating her question in the way I'd originally interpreted it. *Was* I happy with my decision when it came to Logan and Aaron? It hardly took a beat for me to answer that question confidently. Yes, even after all these weeks, I believed I'd made the right choice.

This time when I left the dance that night, I didn't leave

confused and conflicted. I left happier than I'd ever felt in my life. When I dressed in my pajamas that night and curled up with Parrot on my bed, it was in that moment that I realized I was finally whole.

ABOUT THE AUTHOR

Alicia Rades is a USA Today bestselling author of young adult and new adult paranormal fiction. When she's not dreaming up magical stories, she's either binge-watching Netflix, meditating, or spending time with her family. She has an unhealthy obsession with psychic characters and writes with a deck of tarot cards next to her computer.